ATOM

Also by Steve Aylett

Slaughtermatic
The Crime Studio
Bigot Hall
Toxicology
The Inflatable Volunteer

ATOM

STEVE AYLETT

A PHOENIX HOUSE BOOK
Weidenfeld & Nicolson

For Dad

First published in Great Britain in 2000 by Phoenix House

A CIP catalogue record for this book is available
from the British Library

ISBN 1 861591 24 1

Typeset at The Spartan Press Ltd,
Lymington, Hants
Printed in Great Britain by
Clays Ltd, St Ives plc

Phoenix House
An imprint of Weidenfeld & Nicolson
The Orion Publishing Group Ltd
Orion House
5 Upper St Martin's Lane
London WC2H 9EA

Contents

'Well, folks, you'll soon see a baked Appel.'

George Appel,
about to be executed in the electric chair (1952)

1

Atom and Drowner

The city sprawled like roadkill, spreading more with each new pressure. A grey rain slicked Campag Street – cars slewed through smoke and collided with pieces of the Brain Facility. Little flames dotted the rubble like Zippos in a darkened stadium.

Cradling a guilty treasure, Harry Fiasco stumbled through diced masonry. Squadcar cherry lights strobed his eager face. I'm number one, he thought. I'm the business. Look at me walkin' away without even a dent in my hair.

The cold prize steamed as if awakening.

This was no time to be caught with his style round his ankles.

News on the car TV showed flarelit afterscenes of last night's blowup at the City Brain Facility, 'where hundreds of famous brains,' beamed the newsgirl, 'including that of comedian Tony Curtis, were kept on ice. What. A. *Mess.*' Stock shots of missiles. 'The UN Report on Nuclear Deconstruction estimates that thanks to multilateral efforts there are only enough atomic weapons to destroy the world *five* times over instead of eight – way to go!' The President in a storm of flashbulbs. 'In a hastily arranged press conference, the President, due to visit Beerlight in four days, shrugged off accusations of bestiality following publication of a photograph in which he is seen to be kissing a dog.'

The sound came up on the conference. '. . . form of affection. I love him like a brother—'

'Homicides up by nine hundred per cent. And fashion setter Buckyball Tripwire says dresses will be worn drenched in blood this summer. Riot forecast – late morning a few rumbles and a little hail with cops breaking through in the afternoon and a scorcher of an evening due to a high pressure front on the lower east—'

'Enough of this tomfoolery.'

The screen shot to a dot, fading.

Rain glinced the windshield and drool-light ran down the face of Mr Turow. He was a toad-eyed shorty with tar hair and a string-thin tie. He gave creepy-teutonic as rain drummed the tin roof. 'See the building across the street, Joanna? The old brownstone.'

The giant in the driver's seat stirred. His head was a dough mound into which a set of human features had been timidly pressed. The head rotated to look across the carsplash street.

'On the fourth floor are the offices of Mr Taffy Atom. Look at this calling card.'

The giant took the card, which in his hand looked like a postage stamp on a side of beef. He read haltingly. 'Taffy . . . Atom . . . pri - vate . . . defective.'

'Detective, you fool – what kind of idiot would advertise himself as a *defective*?'

'What's dah "p" word mean?'

'According to the Candyman,' Turow leaked, 'and he is the most educated gentleman of my acquaintance, it means to hide your activities even if they are innocent. One of the most perverse products of your sick American culture, it was finally forbidden only a short while ago.

This man Atom must be brave indeed to use it on his advertising. It means he will value results more than appearances, will not be restrained by the rules and at all costs will avoid attention.' Turow simmered in satisfaction. 'All of which is good news for us.'

'There ain't no number.'

'Nor an address – another good sign. Atom is as accomplished and inconspicuous as an ant lifting an eyelash. Take the money and go.'

The giant opened on to the rain and heaved out, then leant back in at Turow. 'What if he don't bite?'

Turow gave indulgent. 'Joanna, you will learn – in this town, everybody bites.'

Atom was a noir silhouette against Venetian blinds, and he knew it. He'd sustained this posture for nearly three hours, in a not-doing meditation to the inner Tao.

The buzzer went and Atom reacted with the flicker of an eyelid. He'd have to start over. 'That figures,' he muttered, then hit the release switch to the outer door.

He leaned back in the dark and contemplated the spritzing of the rain, the bubbling of the fishtank.

Joanna lumbered through the waiting room, which contained a single lawn chair. Three walls were stark white – the fourth was a vast, garishly intense painting of a bridegroom going batshit berserk in a fish market. A load of other stuff in there, crowded around. Joanna passed it by – he got the creeps off art – and pushed through the inner door to darkness.

Someone was sat there, a shape against the blinds, still and silent.

'You Taffy Atom?'

'So I've always been led to believe.'

3

Satisfied, Joanna closed the door. 'I'm Joanna – er, Jo, I mean . . . Joe . . . Joe Aniseed.'

'Joe Aniseed,' the darkened figure repeated without inflection.

'Mind if I siddown?'

'If that's the way you wanna play it.'

'Real dark in here.' Joanna felt his way to a seat across the desk from Atom, and eased down. 'You gonna draw dem blinds?'

'Not on your nelly.'

'Can't see your face.'

'Well it's chiselled, aquiline, even feral,' stated the deep voice, 'with eyes like steel ingots trembling on the smelter rim.'

'Right. Right . . .' To his right a fish tank was bubbling unlit. Joanna felt uncomfortable, like that time he got hit by a car and everyone stared at him. 'Hey, you got fish in the tank, right? I take a look, put a light on?'

'I don't like lightbulbs. Their mystery makes me kinda edgy. I can never tell what's goin' on inside. They constitute a lifeform. Gas. Electrical impulses. Death. Even a body for disposal, Mr *Aniseed*. They perch like spiders on the wall – watching.'

'Gee, I . . . guess I ain't thought much about that.'

'There'll be hell to pay, I promise you.'

So that was what the Candyman called the 'pleasantries' out of the way. So far so good. Down to business. 'Dah reason I'm here, Mr Atom, is I got a problem. I'm needin' to talk to a guy called Harry Fiasco.'

'Fiasco. Ain't he one of Eddie Thermidor's boys?'

'Sure, the mob – he worked on that big somethin' they did, that whattya-call-it—'

'Massacre.'

'Nail on the head, Mr Atom. So the deal is I had a thing

with Fiasco's girl Kitty Stickler, who kinda dances and stuff. And I figured after a while I oughta ventilate Fiasco before he ventilates me. Like math, right? So I tail the guy. Tinder Street. Steam risin' outta the streetholes, that kinda stuff. Dark, you know? So I'm in range and I let rip.'

'So whattya want, a receipt for the bullet?'

'Well it's kinda embarrassin', Mr Atom – but I kinda missed the guy and he ran as fast as his arms and legs could take him. Now he's hidin' out – but see, Mr Atom, I ain't seein' Kitty no more. And Fiasco bein' one of the mob's boys, I don't wanna get found in the weeds or somethin', so I wanna get to Fiasco and tell him it's all square somehow. And I got ten thousand smackers here says you'll find him before I can say somethin' interestin'.'

Joanna felt real chuffed at having got through the pitch, but there was no immediate response from Atom – only the muffled rain and the broiling aquarium.

'So er . . . so whattya thinka my story, Mr Atom?'

'It's got potential and nothing else, bignose.'

'Eh? Hey, you don't understand, they got it in for me, I'm countin' ten in Italian here!'

'Keep counting.'

Three emergency plans occurred to Joanna, but they were the same one painted three colours. 'What about ya partner?' he bellowed like a stunned bull. 'I see that other name on the door out there – Atom and Drowner. Drowner your partner, right?'

'Ms Drowner is my technical adviser – she works from home.'

'So who's gonna help me, your goddamn goldfish?' shouted Joanna, standing – the chair clattered backward against the door. 'Hey, you ain't moved a muscle, yuh weirdo, answer me! You ain't even lookin' at me! God dammit I'm hittin' the lights!' And he lumbered at the door, smacking a wallstud – the lights fizzled up to clinical intensity.

Atom was as he'd described himself, sat languid at his desk, regarding Joanna without expression. But something was wrong with the picture.

'Hey.' Joanna pointed helpfully. 'Hey, you ain't wearin' no *clothes.*'

'Should I be.'

'What if a lady walks in here?'

'That's a matter for the authorities.'

The fishtank glooped – Joanna saw that it too had been illuminated, a sickly green. In the flux of refraction hung a venomous fish the size of a bulldog – in one visual gulp Joanna got the deep body, black and red striped bellyskin, venting gills, streamer fins, high backblade, hinged razor barbs, blunt head and forward eyes. But the snub face looked to have been grafted on. It was human, made over with shutter eyelids and a mouthful of needle-teeth. The specimen yawed slow in the rippling light, showing off the clench and unclench of a gas bladder and the luminescent phosphene ghosts in its silver scales. On the speckle-stone seabed sat a miniature castle. The fish's blue eye gave the scary stare of intelligence.

'Wha' kinda goldfish is *that* it's a goddamn monster!'

With a thrash the fish stuck its expression out of the water and snarled through the clenched grid of its mouth. 'Define your terms, meathead.'

Joanna's bulk wired with shock. 'It's talkin' semantics!'

The tank seemed to explode – the fish was upon him. Poison pain shot up his arm as the predator bit him to the bone.

Joanna heard himself shrieking like a woman, pleading for release, forming words which held meaning only for those who'd dare join him in the rarefied realm above his pain threshold. He hurled himself through exploding furniture. Amid an eyewall skyburst of nerve stars he saw Atom glance from his perusal of the phonebook. 'Mind the furniture, you two.'

'Get him off me! I'm in hell! This! Is! *Hell!*'

Joanna threw off the fiend, which lay gulping on the carpet. 'I'm on the floor, Taffy! I hate the floor!'

Atom stood, affronted. 'Don't you know assaulting a security officer is a federal offence?'

'Security officer?' gasped Joanna, reeling. 'It's a piranha, man! Bit my arm!'

'Count yourself lucky, pal,' queased the fish in its synthetic voice. 'Gemme off the floor, Taff – spit on my gills someone I can't breathe down here!'

'Jed Helms is a credit to his species,' Atom stated, stepping from behind the desk.

'It ain't duty Taff, I was hungry is all.'

Atom retrieved the fish, spreading its pectoral fins. 'All the best operatives are hungry – you're in peak condition.' He dumped the beast into the tank. It sculled languidly to the bottom, its eyes closing. Atom turned his fierce attention to Joanna.

Joanna staggered backward, clutching his arm. 'Now don't come near me you sonofabitch! This place is crazy – you *both* crazy!'

The wall-shadow behind Atom seemed to swell with malevolence as Atom declaimed, 'You swan in here mouthing off about your phony name, your phony predicament, your phony pants, all the while telling me how *I* should dress – then you torture my colleague Jed Helms almost beyond his attention span. Get the hell out of here, or so help me I'll . . .'

'What is wrong now with that *imbecile*?' thought Turow

as he saw Joanna slam out of the building and wheel toward him through the rain.

Joanna tore open the door and stuck his head in. 'Drive, Dumpy, drive – there's monsters in dah house!'

'What?' Turow spat as Joanna crammed himself into the car – he plucked the key from the ignition before Joanna could turn it, and held it behind him as the giant made a grab. 'Calm down you fool, you'll attract attention!'

'He didn't bite, Mr Turow – but looka dis toothmark.' And he displayed what looked like the bite radius of a young shark, arced on his arm. 'Don't go in there, Dumpy.'

'Scared of a little yappy dog or something, a brute like you,' Turow sneered. 'And don't call me Dumpy – stay here while I do a man's work as it *should* be done.' He unlocked and pushed out of the car, scuttling through the rain to the brownstone.

In the lobby he smartened himself up, then entered the elevator. Joanna probably called on some old woman whose only companion was a spaniel temperamental in the head. Simple enough. Fourth floor.

Well, all right, the place was a little creepy but was this not America land of the free? Let them have their dim wallpaper and dense doors.

Everything cruised around his own movements as he walked the hallway, so dreamlike he looked down to check for rollers. Microdread pinwheeled over the carpet, approaching him like a tide. His hair strained to stand on end, curling to question marks under its freight of grease.

Here was the door – ATOM AND DROWNER stencilled on blurglass. He rang the bell and after a pause the door burst open like an exit wound, gusts of methane clouding past him.

He stepped into the waiting room, which was a sky churning with fire and sonic explosions. Igniting magnesia stained the air and wind ripped expectation into ribbons. Here were heavens gone astray and panicking like bats, blinding his forehead and releasing a hailstorm of crisis. 'Mr Atom?' called Turow above the storm, his clothes ballooning with super-rarefied static. 'Are you available for business?' He knuckled airtrash from his eyes, squinting agog through an atmosphere churning with near release. And the wind redirected, buffing a sight-line through the roiling smog.

A resinous spine and ribs were suspended in midair, levitating in theatrical smoke. And amid the creeping fluorescence, inquisition fumes and white-hot theta flashes boomed a voice as though amplified through 50,000-watt speakertowers. And it said:

'An office is a machine for dying.'

Turow began screeching like a vulture, mouth dry. He saw himself, diaphanous in his lack. This encounter was the very litmus of his courage and his face turned reflex blue. He found himself running, beyond his control. The building spat him out like an olive.

2

The Numb Town

Atom pulled on his pants and took the firepole to the garage. Drove through a dogma pageant, Cockroach Centrefold on the stereo. A bullet licked the paintwork. What happens, he thought, when the hitcher and the driver are equally murderous? Looking at this town with an honest eye was like biting into candy with a mouthful of cavities.

A bricolage block on Crane housed Madison Drowner's apartment. Two guys were sparring on the sidewalk with boxing gloves made of tempera meringue. Passing them, Taffy saw the gloves were actually wooden heads removed from statues of the Virgin Mary.

Upstairs, Maddy ushered him in, walking away. 'How they hanging.'

'Geometrically.'

'And I was just mixing some antifreeze.'

'Guess I could use it. Guess we all could. Jed needs a service.'

'Of all the wild suggestions.'

'Just a torn gill. We had a visitor came asking for it. It's a cliché out there, baby.'

Maddy built a freeze to the sacred dimensions. Sometimes Atom wished he could kiss her brain directly. Her eyes, in defiance of the prevailing trend, were open. She was an angel as real as the bones in her body. 'You're warped, Taff. All that glee – it ain't healthy.'

Atom took the glass of blue. 'Health is subjective. I believe I'm evolving.'

'Sure – into a dead man.'

'Where's your imagination?'

'In the medicine cabinet.' She regarded him over a drink. 'You on a prank, Taff? Your forehead's beating like a heart.'

'Sanity's a virginity of the mind, baby. Gimme a shock absorber.' She lit one up between her lips and passed it to him. He breathed it in. 'You know a girl by the name of Kitty Stickler?'

'Sure. Standard-issue blonde. All distinguishing marks removed. Rejects men who never noticed her. Rumours of a brain but nothing conclusive. Sings at the Creosote Palace.'

'That a gun club?'

'All the charm of a live bait store. The chandeliers are rubber – they don't take any chances.'

'Sounds like my kinda venue.'

'Yeah – crash dummy heaven.'

'That's what I'm counting on. The greatest high in this graveyard nation is to have an effect.'

'Effectiveness.' She stood close to him, looking into and through his eyes. 'They got a detox programme for that?'

Atom chuckled. 'You and your wet mouth.' He pensively regarded his gasper. 'I nearly depend on you, baby.'

'You make me laugh,' she said, 'with your threats.'

The Creosote Palace was the last word in public disorder. Espousers of philosophies as diverse as Malraux gathered under one roof to engage in boisterous deceit and explosive arrogance. The only hope of distracting these bastards was to push a bubblehead on stage and get her wailing.

That was Kitty Stickler – up there singing a Beige Kidney standard which listed the surgical assaults all sexes were told they favoured for the female form. She chirped without irony, having undergone every cosmetic procedure on the list. Her body was so media-aligned it barely registered on the retina. She seemed unable to bend. Somewhere was a knot – someday it would give.

Atom entered, reversing the air's ionic charge. Probability statistics polarised. Trying to detect the girl, he refocused until she fuzzed into view, singing like a lollipop. Even at this bandwidth she was like a flashy ad with no trace of a product. Atom strode between the tables, approaching the stage before the flow of his void coat.

'Excuse me, ma'am—'

'Hey!'

'—the name's Atom, I need to ask some questions, in total confidence you understand. You know a guy waves the name Joe Aniseed?'

'What the hell d'you say you are?' Up close she was like a phantom, her face airbrush blurred. 'Get the hell off my stage.'

'You involved with the peltman Harry Fiasco?'

'Ram it up your ass!'

'Just the facts, ma'am.'

The audience were getting attentive, sensing some sort of activity on stage.

'I don't know no Aniseed and I ain't seen Harry for weeks or more – hey Sam, get this shithead off my stage!'

Sam, stripping a chainsaw in the wings, frowned briefly at a disembodied voice.

The crowd perked up as Kitty, powered only by limelight, stalked petulantly off stage.

'Ladies and gentlemen,' said Atom, 'if you'll indulge me. I have assigned a musical note to every grade of human lie.

Here's my rendition of the President's inaugural address.'
And he took out a clarinet.

Dr DeCrow gave cadaverous – except for his mouth, which
bulbed and pupped like a monkey's. Ghoulish as bones in a
canvas bag, he stood by a table lamp for the old uplit mask
effect. 'I deem it a thorough success, Mr Candyman – and
one that has afforded me a great deal of pleasure.'

'That's as may be, sir,' said the fat man in the hotel
armchair. 'What's now required is that we recover the
organ. It cannot be allowed to leave this city.'

'A simple enough task, after all.'

'If there's one thing I've learnt, Doctor, it's that simpli-
city is a blank screen inevitably pelted and abused by the
peanut gallery. Now leave by the back way, sir – I don't
want Turow barging in here and getting into a state.'

The door banged open and Turow hung in, staggering. 'I
am beginning a *nosebleed*,' he cried, then saw DeCrow and
stopped. 'What is *he* doing here?'

'Dr DeCrow was just taking his leave, Mr Turow.'

DeCrow bowed deep. 'Long life,' he crackled, and moved
off, without straightening up. He moved as fast as tables
breed. Passing Joanna at the doorway, he bowed even
lower, and left.

'Why is that creature hanging around?' asked Turow,
shivering. 'He reminds me of one of those insects that
looks dead on the outside.'

'A compelling metaphor, sir – and more fitting than you
know. DeCrow is a man so intelligent he can barely walk
without an interpreter. In any case we decamp shortly for
another hotel. But how went your quest – did the man
Atom welcome our offer?'

Dot-eyed, Turow dabbed his forehead with a scented
kerchief. 'Welcome? Our offer was as welcome as a bat in

a Velcro factory. Atom's place is a devil's funhouse –
Joanna here claims he was bitten by a dog and I am inclined
to believe him. I tell you we were confronted with nothing
but tomfoolery. We left in some hurry – my honour
insulted, you understand. This feeble-minded idiot
thought it would be wise to leave the car and run while it
was still on the move.'

The Candyman released a blubbery laugh. 'Now there's
an idea. To refrain from fulfilment is to let life escape you,
eh Joanna? Close the door and rest yourself.'

'And he went off down some side-alley,' Turow continued, 'and I have been hunting for him like a parent after a
runaway.' He fell into a chair as Joanna closed the door. 'I'd
half a good mind to leave him, but I . . . cannot drive.'

The Candyman consulted a fob-watch, chuckled a little
and replaced it in his jacket. 'Well then. Not a success. But
eloquence, like a honeycomb, is gnawed for pleasure, not
learning. The details, Mr Turow, elude me.'

'Details?' Turow repeated, straining forward, elbows
leant on his knees. He seemed to be undergoing some
inner struggle. Finally he buried his face in his kerchief
and shook his head.

'Joanna, then – sit down, my boy. And tell me your
impression of this man Atom.'

Joanna lumbered forward and settled his huge bulk on to
a tiny wooden dining chair. His face opened like a pit in a
nimbus cloud.

'Wiseguy,' he rumbled.

ATOM'S JOURNAL

*Here's the way I see it. A skeleton with a needle and
cotton. It lives in a house filled with anchors and flame-
throwing equipment. Outside, a threading blizzard.
Authority like a scorpion in a monster truck. Exhausted*

denizens lank as locked boxers. God's massive shell discarded at the edge of the universe. All that's missing is a raven with a plan behind its hard eyes.

3

We've Been Courteous

'These words poison my life.'

Eddie Thermidor liked to think of the mob network as a Frankenstein's monster, more sensitive than its creator. It was, but that wasn't saying much. Born with a glass eye, he became the sort of driver who was oblivious to anyone coming the other way. Now that he had a snorting stable of chauffeurs this attitude informed his business affairs. No one had done so much to redeem the use of flamethrowers up close.

He was sat at a heavy marble table in a stone hall. Thermidor's gang fort was no apartment knock-through like Betty's midtown – this here was custom-built, the outer walls so thick they took up more groundspace than the inner chambers. Industrial gothic was tempered by Bren Shui, the art of exchanging negative energy with the environment through the correct placement of firearms around the home.

He replaced the receiver, the brittle slam echoing. 'Sammy Transam on the tumbler,' he said. 'Says someone sorta took over the chaos at the Creosote.'

Nada Neck and Shiv were sat on a low couch by the wall. Three creases appeared in Nada Neck's forehead – one for each nerve impulse. 'Didn't Transam used to go round sellin' insulation in the form of codeine? Perhaps it has turned finally upon him.'

'So his brain's flipped like a flounder? I'll push him off a roof so tall he'll be dead o' boredom before he hits the sidewalk.'

Shiv examined the set of ratchet knives which rested open on his knees. 'I take him. Wet one of these here thinnies.'

'Shiv Shiv Shiv. I'm touched. Hear that, Neck? Artist inspired. Flurry o' knifework and your guts unspool to the carpet. Salt the blade before lunging probably. Hold that thought, Shiv, okay? Kitty was on – I want her in here ready to salute the floorboards.'

'Uh, she's downstairs, boss, she's here,' said Nada Neck.

'What? What do I need Kitty Stickler in my life?'

'You said you wanted her here.'

'On my order, not turnin' up like this is some village coffeehouse for the talkin' about of flowers and bunny rabbits, eh?'

'Sorry, boss, you've lost me.'

'Shiv thinks,' whispered Shiv without looking up, 'that Neck only plays dumb.'

Kitty started stamping her heels and everyone noticed she was in the room.

'Kitty – to what in the devil's plan do I owe the pleasure?'

'Salute the floorboards, huh?' She went over to a table and tore a shocker out of the pack, lighting up. ' "These words poison my life!" You know I nearly died today?'

'That an inconvenience in your case?'

'Oh ha ha, you think it's the true fun bein' there haranguin' slobs from that stage?'

'Sure, it's all we talk about round here – whether yours is the true fun. If it'd be the same for those of us with movin' parts.'

Kitty stalked up to the heavy table, gripped its corners and glared across it into Thermidor's one living eye. 'You've shot up in my estimation, Eddie – like when they discovered the brontosaurus could sit back on its ass.'

Thermidor stuck out his jaw like the tray of a cash register. 'Well now, this is real read-all-about-it factual information you're givin' me, Kitty. A man like me just might not be able to find room for it in his life.'

'Okay, okay.' She sat down opposite, smoking. 'Guy comes in real easy, gets up onstage and starts in on me with the threats et cetera. Then we got verbal abuse, playin' the flute, flawfire, the woiks. Bullets everywhere – got a nick in my makeup, see?'

'I can't see nuthin.'

'Well it hurts, Eddie.'

'You don't know what hurt is. Your marrow's never seen daylight.'

'Yeah? Well looky here, Mister Been-There-Stole-the-Shirt.' Kitty swung a long leg on to the table and pulled up her pants leg, gesturing with a cigarette. 'See there? Bonesaw, straight the way through. Two inches height added, stuck back together, end of story.'

'Kitty, I told you not to show me that stuff. Why do I need scars in my life?'

'It's a real doozy,' Shiv hissed, looking over her shoulder.

'Jesus,' Kitty yelped, hiding the scar, 'how long he been standin' behind me? Gives me the creeps.'

'Siddown, Shiv.' Thermidor watched as Shiv slithered back to the couch. 'Now Kitty, I hear tell you got into a conversation with the guy – everyone heard it you understand, but I need it from you.'

'Yeah?' Kitty drew nervously at the shocker. 'Okay. Said his name was Atom? Adam? Somethin'. Gumshoe modality. Said he was lookin' for Harry. Fiasco.'

'Well that's funny – why'd he ask you, Kitty? Got somethin' goin' on with Fiasco?'

'Sure, he wishes,' said Kitty, killing her shocker and getting up. 'Well, it's been a fun visit, Eddie. I've registered my complaint.'

'You sorry I got you the gig?'

'No no no, Eddie, grateful I *am* but it ain't too classy. And gettin' private dicks flyin' on to the stage?'

'Take it as a compliment, Kitty. Oh and hey. You know where I might find Fiasco?'

'Uh-uh,' she replied at the door.

'Now why don't I believe you?'

'Ho-mo-sexial panic?'

And she was gone.

Thermidor pondered a moment. 'So who's this Adam Atom guy?'

'Only guy in the PI modality with a name like that's Taffy – Taffy Atom.'

'That's good, Neck. Whatta we know about him?'

'Heard he grew a moustache on his stomach,' hissed Shiv.

'What about you?' he asked Nada Neck.

'Yeah, what he said boss, I heard that too.'

'Uh-huh. And that's it, eh?'

'Ain't that enough?'

Thermidor leant back and regarded the two. 'Nada Neck, you are a fine right arm but your philosophy cannot be spoken aloud without lapsing into an Australian accent. Shiv, you are a fine knifeman but you have an interest in knives which leads you into errors of judgement.'

The two shifted on their seat. Shiv would have liked to mention the boss's weakness for a certain blonde bubblehead. This he felt was inappropriate. Shiv considered that he himself was the better match. After all, Kitty was a scalpel addict and he was a blademan. He understood such joys. You haven't lived till you've operated on your own arm.

'Tell you what,' Thermidor announced. 'Shiv – put a tail on Kitty, see if she leads you to the boy Fiasco. Nada Neck – you find me Atom. He knows somethin' about Vanishin' Harry, I wanna know. Get outta here.'

'Shiv will do good work,' buzzed the knifeman as he and Nada Neck backed out of the room.

'Kitty, Kitty, Kitty,' murmured Thermidor.

Fiasco, Atom. Their bones would pop in a rendering mill before they interfered again with that pure girl.

What was the hook? The strutting, the selfishness, the sarcasm. She was the very phantom of his mother.

Even if the boss thought he was exaggerating, Transam knew what he'd witnessed. He'd got through stripping his chainsaw and that swab baby – the one no one could ever quite see – was stood there trying to get his attention. And looking out, he found there was a stranger on stage wearing this huge black coat and playing a giant flute. And as he played, something began to inflate from the end of the instrument. It was a human head, resembling exactly that of the musician, its lips attached to this end of the flute and facing its twin. Then the body began to tumble from beneath the head like a birthing calf. The feet hit the stage and the form filled out, swaying slow in the ventilation. Then the arms quickly inflated, quivering up into position, and the real guy, the first one, detached and floated out above the audience. The new man, coat and all, had taken over on the flute, and his music bobbed and drifted like the airborne figure. The floating man, uplit and shadow-freaked, was screaming as though terrified, and so was everyone else. The clientele began to fire at the ceiling, at each other, at the musician on stage. A Barrett 82 whooped off, detaching one of the rubber chandeliers, and by the time it thumped to the deck, everyone had drawn.

The musician reacted weirdly. As the volleys flew, he telescoped the flute and drew his coat all around like Bela Lugosi, sinking behind it and turning his back. It looked like the ammo was disappearing into that coat like pledges into a manifesto. Then when a shell burst the floating man, next thing the whole joint was being showered with confetti, all these louts looking up like it was Christmas, and the stage guy was nowhere.

Every single flake of confetti bore a miniature likeness of the stranger's face.

4

The Black Burden

There was only one venue worse than the Creosote Palace and that was the Delayed Reaction Bar on Valentine Street, a dim pit of cawing rooks, glass dust and layered distortion. Those who asked for a shot and a beer never lived to examine the beer. Don Toto the barman sold anarchy symbols made of baked wheat – pretzels, he called them. The clientele guzzled drugs laced with gin, world ales, soda and even milk. Some cocktails would cause their heads to swell up so they looked like Newt Gingrich. These unfortunate ones had to be rounded up and slaughtered like hogs. Behind the bar hung a framed photo of Roni Loveless, the boxer who, ordered to throw a fight, burst through an inner struggle to beat not only his opponent but everyone in the arena and its locality in an outward-blooming explosion of violence against suppressive mediocrity.

Flea Lonza sat under the wind turbine nursing a Sniper's Delight. An oily corpse in a casual jacket, he shored up his withered senses by smuggling facts and tobacco into America. His ears were just big enough to laugh at. In his capacity as a double edge only one client paid him to give the word to other people – and that client had just sat opposite.

'You inform on me lately, Flea?'

'When don't I?'

'You ain't holdin' out on me are you?'

'Ever get confused, Atom?'

'No.' Atom lit a shock absorber. 'Smoke?'

Flea flashed his jacket to show a hundred shock boxes like the back room of an old cigar store. 'Devil need a match?'

'I'm asking the questions – you recommend my services the last few days?'

'Yeah. Big guy. Dumb. Took a half-hour to select his name. But the little slimeback with him – he did the real talkin'. Asked about Fiasco too – I coulda sent 'em straight to Harry but I put 'em on to you.'

'Thanks.' Atom handed over five hundred smackers.

'This kinda money could get me into trouble, Atom.'

Atom drew on his gasper. 'Don't knock it. Trouble'll never leave you, never consider you unworthy of attention. Trouble's a saint. Your saint, Flea.'

Right away Atom regretted it – what a terrible thing to say to a friend. Why did he have to be smart always? 'I'm sorry, Flea. Here.' He gave him a pearl-finish photograph of himself sobbing amid a huddle of Emperor penguins. 'And this.' He reached into his coat and retrieved something, unfolding it. 'It's a clip-on charm filter.' He fitted the tin bib on to Flea. 'Now tell me you love me.'

'I hate you, Atom – I only tolerate you because you pay me and buy me presents.'

'See? It's working already. Catch you later, Flea.' Atom got up and left.

A half-minute later a posse of Thermidor's wrecking crew boomed in, headed by Nada Neck. 'We don't want no trouble,' said Toto the barman, and that cracked everyone up. Toto gave a little bow, grinning as he cleaned a glass.

Nada Neck drew a mufflered M61 Persuader sub and

breezed it on to Flea's forehead as he sat down casual and surveyed the bar. Flea reacted like he'd found a bug in his apple. 'You gentlemen need a muscle relaxant?'

'You the local dataroach, right? I think you can help me. Yes, I think so.'

'Look me in the eye and select a topic, if you can.'

'Taffy Atom – you've met him.'

'Sure I know Atom but he's kinda busy. He's a shadow-man.'

'That this week's tag for a gumshoe? What's makin' him so busy? Remember the gun.'

'Some guys want him to find Harry Fiasco.'

'Which guys?'

'Big dumbster and a lavender seed, don't know the names.'

'You don't know a whole lot of anything do you, Roach? That a bib?'

'You can have it – it's a charm filter.'

'Wiseguy, eh?'

'Look, all I know is Fiasco's doin' a job on the side. The galoot said somethin' about a squasher.'

'A squasher.'

'A brain, to you.'

'A brain to me, to me a brain. Ain't that dandy. Okay, Roach, where we find Atom?'

On the way out, Nada Neck stopped at the door. 'There's a time for singing,' he muttered thoughtfully, 'and a time for fighting. Here, time stands still.' And he turned back to the darkness, raised the automatic and let rip at Flea. A thousand Lucky Strikes lit at once.

5

There Goes My Gun

'Some people keep their faces on the inside,' said Taffy. He and Maddy were in the privacy hole she had expanded to contain a gun lab. Resembling an alien's bathroom, this was where Maddy had brought ballistics to a culinary art. The brotherhood were right in their claim that if you kept a weapon you'd soon find an excuse to use it, a theory proven by global atomic peril and their own gunplay. Madison had moved on, alchemising the old practice into liquid gold. Instant-acting psychoactives in a softnose dart put victims seamlessly into a religiously dazzling landscape from which they'd emerge brighter than before. Sleepers froze people where they stood, wiping out three minutes of perception the loss of which was noticed only when bank tellers began shrieking at a sudden and massive financial discrepancy. Treasury members were hit with hemisync inducers while speaking in public, causing them to snigger the truth. Archrivals could be shot and slung into a cab, awaking with no identity at all.

Geared to place more value on property than human life, the law could forgive the lack of death but not the lack of destruction and bent over backwards to promote metabolics from their status of mild assault. Even this rarely stuck as victims awoke feeling better than they had in years. When metabolics hit the streets the users' names became a prized resource and people travelled miles to fling themselves into the firing line. The brotherhood, who regarded ignorance as something close to a moral duty, stuck with simple alloys. Maddy holstered her achievement behind her heart.

'Wanna hear the rest?'

'Don't smoke in here, Taff,' said Maddy. 'Bad for the ammo.'

'What you workin' on?'

Maddy lifted a tin football out of the circuit manipulator. 'Syndication bomb. Strips the subtext from whatever situation it's tripped in. Leaves everything meaningless for up to three hours.'

'Have to trip it on remote.'

'Not if you carry this.' She held out her hand, fist closed.

'What is it?'

She opened her hand, palm up – there was nothing there.

'Nothing there, babe.'

'Just so long as you know that.'

They went out to the front room, where Taffy fixed them both a freeze. Maddy was at the open window, her hair blowing like smoke. Taffy gave her the glass and watched her awhile, her aura pulsing like the borealis. 'Flex and I'm agog, babe. A word and I'm medicated.'

She hadn't heard him. She was looking out over the night. Little shots like firecrackers echoed from the other side of the Triangle. 'I love this city. So many bullets between the people – like a join-the-dot puzzle, you know? All linked together with lead.'

'Just remind me why that's a virtue, baby.'

'Because when so many people have a thing in common, you can yank it like a toilet flush and get back to what really matters.'

'Like what.'
'Come here.'

Nada Neck's Persuader semi-egotistic was an early grid-pulse modified from a Czech M61. It sampled his intent through the grip and placed it at the heart of each shot pellet in the form of a concentrated etheric molecule. In the early enthusiasm for fire-by-wires this was seen as a more direct way of expressing oneself. May I come in? he thought, pulling the trigger, and the door to Atom's office blew to pieces.

The only sound in the darkness was the bubbling of water. The four hoods entered in a flurry of sloped hats and slowed a moment, cautious. 'Room's in negative, Neck,' warned Minuteman. 'It ain't right.'

'Don't like the sounda them bubbles,' said Beefheart and the room exploded into screams and flying glass. Minuteman was firing indiscriminately in the dark, back-flash illuminating his panic and the whirling, indistinct figure of Beefheart, something locked to his face. The figures danced in the gunstrobe like ravers in hell. Everything was distorted, voices expressing views their owners didn't recognise.

Then the smash of a window and reality seemed to stream in, sorting out the air. Nada Neck went over and gazed down at the sidewalk. There was Beefheart, his skull tackle weeded out on the concrete, and next to that flexed an oily fish the size of a steroid arm.

An hour later Atom's phone lit up. 'This is Taffy Atom's answering machine – after the tone, put down the phone. Don't leave a message and don't ever call me again.'
• 'Hey, Atom. We got your fish. Hear me, Atom? We got Jed Helms. Say a few words, Jed.'

'Hey, Atom, it's great here! They got a swimmin' pool and everythin! These guys really know how to live!'

'Eddie Thermidor wants to exchange, Atom. We give you the fish, you give us the brain. Or your little mutant friend gets it.'

• 'Mr Atom, this is Candyman – you've met my associates. I'd like to discuss candidly a matter which will be to our mutual advantage. My tumbled number is under six. I'll be waiting, sir. Good evening.'

• 'Now don't be silly. Ain't you a team player? Use your noodle before it's stripped of membrane, Atom. Have I made up your mind yet?'

• 'Come come, sir. It takes patience to appreciate the wrong reply. Though I possess such a virtue I regret I've not the time to exercise it. I would put Mr Turow on the line but when exasperated his voice matches the 2600 tone and plays merry hell with the connection. Let us look for one quality we both observe. I await your call.'

• 'What is it with you? Don't you know Thermidor'll put you under the bridge? Don't you care if you end up coughing pink lungblood into the grass? You sonofabitch you're gonna go dead with a full set in your back. You're on your last goddamn knees.'

• 'You disappoint me, sir. This affair advances without us, and your unresponsivity resembles too closely a wad of cardboard to present itself with any pride to history. Regret is the broadest frontier. Make your move, sir, or your dental records will have their day.'

• 'I hope you're proud of yourself. Mr Thermidor invites you into his life and you're the wiseacres. The one-man band. Well, a guy like you can make a choice but you ain't tough enough to take it. Tense up – you're headed for hell in a dodgem.'

- 'Atom, it's Toto. Flea's in the hospital, a few burns, be okay. Says thanks for the bib.'
- 'Taff. It's Maddy. Just wanted to hear your voice.'

'You will please to put your hands over your head,' stated Turow two hours later, standing in the office doorway with a girly gun and the bulk of Joanna. 'Put a hurt on him, Joanna.'

'Been expectin' you fellas,' remarked Atom, savouring a shock absorber.

'Expecting us!' Turow gasped. 'I'll tear your face off and use it to blow my nose before you know what's hit you!'

'Naughty naughty, Mister Atom,' said Joanna, grabbing him by the shoulder. 'We takin' you to the Candyman. And then we'll see who's clever, and who's smart.'

6

The Man Who Disappeared

The car reeled off. A window was open. The night smelt of gun metal and old lightning. Atom was blindfold in the back seat with Turow pushing the little flaw into his side. Atom followed their progress over TV news. 'The President, due to visit Our Fair State in three days as part of his campaign on the Victory Without Peace ticket, was seen licking a lizard this morning in what has been described as a public relations disaster.'

Saints Street, Valentine, Prod, Size, Broadcast, Devant . . .

'Technohead Leon Wardial claims to have stolen the mayor's aura. "It's safe in an orgone box but if I don't get five hundred large by midnight it's dispersal time. Oh and by the way, it smells bad." The mayor was too tired to comment.'

Manic, right on Smith, left on String, right on Raissa, past the falling road . . .

'Scientists have found that the gene for low IQ is biologically paired with that of a fondness for pasta.'

Scanner, Plug, Peejay, Kayelef . . .

'And the Beerlight Justice Ring has decided on the site of the planned zero tolerance landfill. The authority, which claims there is no danger of overflow, has selected the hospital south of downtown's Beretta Triangle.'

Through the Portis Thruway to Gerald, right on Brett,

left on Bird. The car drew to a halt, the door opened. 'Bird Street Hotel,' announced Joanna, whipping off the blind-fold.

When they entered the hotel room, Turow walked ahead. He bent down to someone in an armchair, whis-pered something, then stepped aside. The Candyman seemed part of the armchair's design, all polished mono-chrome and formality. He bulged from the background like something viewed through a convex lens. When he spoke it was with a volley of blubbery bonhomie. 'We begin well sir. You have on your trousers. Welcome, and sit you down. A regrettable use of muscle in conveying you here – I apologise on all fours.' But he didn't move, any more than Atom. 'Rough-housing is an inexact science. Why Turow here is convinced you've had some shall we say rowdy visitors, who have left your office the worse.'

'Maybe.'

'Maybe. Hmm. Another interested party?'

'Thermidor.'

'Thermidor.' The Candyman frowned, quiet awhile. 'A pity.' Then he was all smiles again. 'Well, sit you down sir. Come one come all, and I commend you sir – you succeeded in giving Mr Turow the world-class heeby-jeebies. You must tell me anon how you did it. Though I'll wager it would take more than two jaws to speak that species of truth.'

Joanna hung back as subtle as a henge stone and Turow perched in a corner seat. Atom sat on the couch opposite the Candyman, and accepted a drink. 'I'm reluctant to respond to a remark with so many possible implications.'

The Candyman barked with laughter. 'Ah, you're the man for me, sir. It takes one of your calibre to suspect my meaning of a byzantine genealogy hitherto traceable only

34

by myself and a select few other. I wonder if you know how right you are. How close you've come to the shocking facts. A question sir: when your office was sacked, was an object taken? An object of not a little bargaining value?'

'Not a little.'

'Something semi-sentient, technologically sustained.'

'After a fashion.'

'You'll get it for me, sir, at the nearest and dearest opportunity.'

'Since when?'

'Perhaps you doubt my sincerity.'

'Never gave it a thought. But imagine my surprise when Scooter here turned up at the office wearing all his ties at once and trailed by a waterhead with next to no nervous system. That'll put salt in anyone's coffee.'

'Hand on heart, sir, and big as life, I regret the unpleasant necessity. That notwithstanding, here we are, and now is good a time as any to pierce the soft crown of the affair. Are you familiar sir, with the author Franz Kafka.'

'Sure. Greatest black author ever lived.'

'He wasn't black sir.'

'He probably is by now.'

'No matter – as I need scarcely remind you, Kafka was of a most singular personality. Why, he'd think nothing of riding on a hound, or sticking wax lips on his eyeglasses. Seeing the world for what it was, he passed the time by whining with artful care, and an attention to detail which could oxidise completely the face of a lying optimist. He would moan, sir, to a standard unimagined by the canker poets. No amount of fashion and falsehood could conceal man's futility from his eyes. Even before the nearest war, mankind was an experiment repeated long past its demonstrable validity. It was without comfort, use or protection; mean, tarnished and afraid. Like all who have sung such facts, he died denied and bleeding from the lungs. Are you with me so far?'

'I can bite on it.'

'Better and better. Now sir – to look at me, what would you say was my abiding concern? What fires my horizon?'

'At a guess I'd say slobbing.'

'Ha – I can enjoy a joke at my expense sir – don't we all? But there's method to the question. Would you believe me sir, if I told you my fascination in life is with the scurrying ones, those low pests the average man wouldn't think twice about stamping on with a satisfying crunch.'

'Lawyers.'

'You take me literally sir – I admire a man who takes me literally, his word is likely to be worth something. But no – I meant merely that I have an abiding fascination with insects. Hardy handfuls. Were you aware sir, that the brothers McKenna, after whom the square in this fair city is named, guided their hallucinogenic explorations with a humming, buzzing vocal harmonic by which they reckoned to merge with the infospace of giant alien insects, and thus be transformed. And that one of the fifty or so gospels omitted from the New Testament is *Allogenes* – meaning literally "from another race" – where an initiate discovers the power within by intoning and merging with its signatory sound, "zza zza zza".'

'You should get out more, Candyman.'

'You filthy swine!' gasped Turow, darting up from his chair.

'Easy does it, Turow,' said the Candyman mildly. 'Allow our honoured guest to hear me out. Franz Kafka, Mr Atom, was another soul attuned to the universal bandwidth. Just as poor Gregor Samsa found himself thrumming and chirping in a manner unintelligible to human beings, so Kafka was a real tyre-kicking alien.'

'Sure, a true child of the universe.'

'If you consider, as many do, that the universe is a drear drift of superdead ashes.' The Candyman paused, pouring himself a drink. 'Several years ago, I began to hear vague rumours. It was said that the great author's brain had been preserved and, through a provenance I could neither chart nor dismiss from my imagination, was a prized item among collectors. Do you have any conception of its value among those vultures, sir? It fetched more money than war with every change of ownership. As much as JFK's among the miming profession. And I made it my aim to acquire that organ. Wild horses couldn't drag me through a hedge backwards sir, and I traced the brain finally to the cryogenic facility here in Beerlight, where it resided under a bland alias. Turow and Joanna were already in my employ, but for the work at hand I needed a strong arm capable of more than the pulling of a trigger – though Joanna does so with wit and grace, don't you, my boy?'

'Presumably he's let off his leash to vote.'

'Oh, I have every confidence in him. Which is why I sent him with Turow to find a premises man – in a town of Beerlight's reputation it seemed sure they'd be hanging off the fire escapes like grapes from the vine. Harry Fiasco appeared an enterprising youth, a little homicidal round the edges perhaps, keen to exert himself outside the usual family chores. He was not in the habit of doing good. A degree of latitude was allowed him and he took heroic advantage. Not only did his break-in cause a mess to match the Celebration riots but he made off with the prize. The boy has taste and an eye for opportunity. Hats off to Harry Fiasco, sir, that's what I say.'

'Uh-huh,' drawled Atom, pulling a shocker and sparking up. 'So it's a pincer movement, with real pincers.'

The Candyman chortled. 'Exactly, sir.'

Atom shook his head solemnly. 'Not me. Not for a squasher. You'll have to do better than that.'

The Candyman's smile burst like a balloon. He glanced aside at Joanna, then fixed Atom's eye and held up an airstopper between stubby thumb and forefinger. 'Look at this bullet, sir – the lifespan of an aphid, but by gad the changes it can wring. And Joanna here knows how to send it on its way, don't you, my boy?'

Hearing his name, Joanna sniggered low.

'Excuse the interruption,' Atom remarked. 'I need to know if I'm meant to be gettin' scared soon.'

'Why are we wasting time with this imbecile?' Turow snapped, agitated. 'Tell Joanna to knife him carefully and we can deal with Thermidor face to face.'

'You must excuse Mr Turow, sir – an impulsive fellow whose happiest moment was finding a garter snake in the mail.'

'Shall I ventilate him, Mr Candyman?' asked Joanna, his tongue lolling.

'Really, Joanna, calm yourself. Watch Joanna as he thinks thoughts as vast and slow as empires, Mr Atom. That foam about his mouth is the cream of worldly wisdom. Now where were we?'

'We were discussing a bullet. It seems I was gonna have the pleasure of its presence in my heart.'

The Candyman gave a blubbery laugh. 'By gad you are a fellow, sir, that you are. I can barely keep my eyes off you. An extraordinary character.'

'You don't get it, do you?' squeaked Turow in exasperation.

'Turow!' barked his master.

Turow stood seething with weakness.

The Candyman turned to Atom. 'Now, sir, about the brain – I've hunted it from Prague to Tangiers to the antique avenues of New Orleans. And now that I'm this close I'll have it by every means at my disposal.'

'Disposal being the operative word.'

'Crime is an evolving definition, sir,' the Candyman stated, his face slack. 'And one must evolve with the times.'

7

Homecoming

'The gent's a real high-wire talker,' Atom told Madison as they strolled the hospital. 'Icy pedigree. Anglo. Big guy but a falling blossom'd gash his cheek. Tried selling me on some transcendence deal but there were more holes in his story than a sex doll. It's taking a weird course.'

'Don't worry about Jed, Taff. He's the one that got away.'

'You got a portable circuit-cooler? Mob ain't likely to provide the necessary maintenance and we don't want him overheating. Remember when he got in the tropical tank behind the bar at the Cerys Club?'

'Sure. Those Japanese fighting fish never stood a chance. But red suited the decor.'

They entered Flea's room to find him in audience with the Caere Twins. 'Hello, shadowboy, hello, datagirl,' the two said in unison. These bottle-bald cuties weren't natural twins but accidental clones. The original Caere girl had left a blood trace at a crime scene and the cops set up a polymerase chain reaction to increase exponentially the quantity of testable DNA. The technician was kidnapped and the reaction left to run for a month, resulting in a whole new girl who fought her way out of the precinct.

'Beware this grinner and her doppelganger, Flea, they'll tear off a ball each, stuff them up your nostrils and punch you in the nose.'

'Really?' Flea asked, brightening and sitting up.

'Flea's a candidate, Mr Taffy,' said the Twins, pushing Atom and Madison out. 'In quarantine.' The Twins were crime stylists who got off on the coining of new offences. They'd gone to the hospital suspecting the intersect of Nada Neck's etheric and Flea's bib generated a fresh violation. They weren't after some benign act fallen foul of a legislation twitch or an old trespass enhanced to the fashion, but a wholly new and original template, outside the seven sins.

'Between breaking a window and paving a nation,' the Twins chanted, 'harsh is the story.'

The door slammed behind Atom and Drowner. Invulnerable as smoke, Madison drew a shock as they started away. 'That how they dismissed you when you were an item?'

'I don't choose to recall.'

'You can't hide from me, Taff. I hear they had you out like a worker bee.'

Atom matched her. 'I was young, I needed the honey.'

'I'll admit they're sweet. Geared up?'

'Hand's recharging in the core,' said Atom, slightly abashed. 'You wouldn't be holding would you baby?'

Madison pulled something from her coat – it looked like an old powder compact. Time bomb.

Eyes so close together they merged like a double yolk, Shiv followed Kitty Stickler through the rain. At one point he'd lost her in front of a mannequin display, but the blade of his knife quivered her way like a compass needle. He ached to gentle the shaft in her silken heart. 'I'm not like the others,' he whispered. 'I can see you – all the time.' She was a real doll – knock her down and her eyes would close. 'Will you cry real tears, Kitty?' he hissed, and crossed the road toward her.

Jed Helms was slapping discordantly along the keyboard of a black piano. 'Hey, Thermidor, what am I doin?' He kept right on. 'What's this, eh? What am I doin'?'

Thermidor stared back.

'Practisin' my scales,' shouted Helms. 'Eh? *Practisin' my scales!*' And he splashed into laughter.

'Why do I need this?' said Thermidor, turning to Nada Neck. 'Why do I need fish playin' piano in my life?'

'You mean "piano-playin' fish", boss.'

'Neck, I respect you as a man but as a hitman you elude me. What happened to gun karma? I'll be a clean skeleton before I hang my life on a fire-by-wire. What is it with you and softshooters, uh? Slugs with little minds inside? What else they got – go-faster stripes? Special bullets for victims with flyaway hair? Why don't you buy from Gat Shack like Carl Banoffi?'

'Banoffi's a grunt.'

'Ask a grunt about cause and effect, Neck, he'll surprise you. I'm sendin' Carl after the guy with the PI modality. Call it a weakness. I'm walking away now.'

Banoffi shadowed Atom down String Street toward Valentine. Today he favoured a Harry Magnum to the right and a Bulldog Special to the left – these were woo cannons in .44 without even a recognition grip, though he'd toned the recoil on the Harry so he wouldn't spin clockwise when he fired both. The knuckles of Banoffi's right hand were tattooed with the word KNUC and those of the left were inscribed KLES. His mother had believed the way to teach little Carl to read was to tag the name to the object. His forehead said FOREHEAD and his chin said CHIN and so on. Even his eyelids were inscribed, though how he was expected to see this was a mystery to many. Banoffi told people he could neither read nor appreciate their laughter, ever.

He put his rage at the service of the mob but secretly feared that this misplacement would one day overbalance him into a pit of inescapable regret. Without inspiration he raised the Magnum and Charter at Atom's back, and noticed that Atom had dropped something – looked like a powder compact. The sidewalk went up like a bullet through a biscuit.

The compact was a two-hour loop mine, which cycled the victim through the same few hours repeatedly until a pre-set release point. Before time manipulation went underground these had been developed by the cops as a means of entrapment – finding that the weight of their actions was erased with the actions themselves, even the mildest citizen would soon explode into a reckless frenzy of rampaging mayhem. Mines set for a mere dozen cycles would do the trick and then time would be allowed to proceed, the arrested suspect laughing wildly in the belief that time would skip back again in a moment.

Carl Banoffi, however, had made a lively career of such mayhem, firing his own body weight in bullets every day. When he found himself back at the Fort being told to oblong the gumshoe, and when two hours later he found himself there again, and again, he began to implode. 'Boss, I am growing tusks trying to off him,' he sobbed.

'I have only just told you to do so,' Thermidor frowned. 'Are you the full dime, Carl Banoffi?'

Carl went for a walk in O'Hara Park and was sat on a bench watching the birdies when he found himself back at the Fort being told to ventilate Atom. This went on and on. Sometimes Carl never bothered with Atom and ate lunch at the Nimble Maniac. Sometimes he cracked wise to Thermidor or said his words along with him. Once he shot Thermidor. Once he even shot Atom. Another time he did a walkabout, slaying everyone in the Fort. It bored hell out of him. One time he got shot by Nada Neck, and after a blank little while found himself being ordered by Thermidor to off Atom.

He started going to the Muse Street movie house to see the end and beginning of *The Yawn – Bane of the Vampire*, knowing not only what was going to happen in the movie but in the theatre and most of the surrounding area. After three hundred cycles he knew the assigned two hours pretty well and was no longer irritated by the regular recall to the moment of Thermidor's order – he would just wander out in the midst of it and return to what he was doing. He never saw the middle of *Bane*.

But he could pick up a book at any point and right near the Fort was the Chain Street Library. During the next two hundred cycles he devoured three books, leaving the Fort every two hours and strolling down to pick up exactly where he'd left off. One was Eddie Gamete's *Punching the Sarge*, in which Gamete speaks of 'the carefree invulner-ability they assure us we felt as children, contrary to our accurate memory of the time'. The next was *The Ultimate Diet*, a study of cadaver decomposition rates. And thirdly there was Leon Wardial's *Freeload Velocity*, in which the protagonist is mere anatomy moved by terror – 'Give me any general statement,' Wardial concluded, 'and I'll refine it to disgrace.' This stuff had squirly parameters – it hogged his imagination. He was laughing and didn't know why.

'I want you to ventilate Atom,' said Thermidor for the thousandth time.

'You're not a happy man, boss – I see that. Did you ever just sit with your lady and watch a tree?'

'You're tellin' me what – what?'

'Universal fear flakes away like the enamel off a spud-gun, you know? Immensity is less reproach than dismissal.'

'Nada Neck – gimme a gun. Now.'

Banoffi was down at the harbour handling intertidal sea jellies when the bomb ended. It had been set for two thousand cycles. He had spent half a year in loop time.

He laughed, marvelling at his ability to leave town. He wrote a book. The work was rejected, his rage was redirected and he became his own man. A year after his release from the timeloop, twenty publishing houses across America were blown to smithereens.

8

Horse Feathers

Atom arrived at the Fort with flowers and a sack of ants. He was shown into the marble hall, where Thermidor was dining at the far, far end of the table. Disposable flunkeys stood at the wall.

'Mr Atom. Welcome to my life. Nada Neck – put the flowers in water. In the furnace dump the ants. Minuteman – take and sell Mr Atom's coat. And check him for flaws.'

Minuteman removed Atom's coat and patted him down. 'He's flawless, Mr Thermidor.'

'I been askin' round about you, gumshoe,' said Thermidor as Minuteman left. 'Hear you got some kinda pun gun'll charm the cats outta their pyjamas. You're a smart one, Atom, I could tell right away.' The clanking of cutlery echoed in the otherwise silent chamber. Thermidor had not looked up since Atom entered. Now he stopped. 'What is this, a tomato? Comedians. What is this? Why do I need tomatoes in my life?' Thermidor picked up the tomato and brandished it. 'Who put this goddamn tomato in my life? Silencer – get the chef in here.'

The plate scraped like chalk as Thermidor pushed it away. He regarded the tomato thoughtfully. 'Ever peeled your pants off over slicked blood, Atom?'

'Not in this lifetime.'

'Hold that thought.' He looked at Atom. 'You know kids are spoilt these days – there's an infinite number of opinions to ignore. Loyalty – real, read-all-about-it loyalty – that's rare as white gold. Harry Fiasco – well. But Carl Banoffi, Carl I know is a good boy – I'd barely begun stating my requirement to off you when he left without a word, as if he knew my heart. I could use more like him in my life. What did you do to him?'

'Guess I threw him for a loop.'

'That's kinda elliptical.'

'I saw him down at the docks, boss,' said Nada Neck, re-entering, 'holdin' a jellyfish up to the light.'

'Those ants good and burnt? I don't want ants in my life. Little invaders. See what I found in the food, Neck?'

'Tomato.'

'Good boy. We havin' fun yet, Atom?'

'Can't say.'

'Well, you damn well *better* say. Eh?' He stared at Atom awhile, then looked to the ceiling. 'Boy, this is gonna be tough.'

The chef was led in by the blunt-faced Silencer. 'Well look who it ain't,' said Thermidor as the guy was pushed down into a chair. 'Servin' me tomatoes. Cute as a dog on a paddle steamer. Where'd you learn to do that, fryboy?'

Ashen-faced, the chef was silent.

Thermidor sauntered over. 'You know Korova used to fire employees like blanks, but not me. I know how it is. Your hat says one thing, your head says another. I don't need explanations or apologies. Just refresh my ailing memory. Why would anyone in their right head eat a tomato?'

When the chef spoke it was like something whispered in the bowl of a radar dish. 'Grief?' he ventured.

'Eh? I hear you say "grief"? The sky was the limit for a

minute there and that's what you pull down? What now, you want I should roll over like a Corvair? Let me guess – you like tomatoes?'

Thermidor took the tomato from the table, cupped his face to remove his glass eye, and squashed the tomato into the empty socket. Squatting down before the chef, he smiled. 'Look into my eye,' he said, and the chef raised his head to view the glistening pulp. 'Be my guest. Tuck in. It's smart food, right? Got real brains behind it.' He pushed his face close to the twitching chef's. 'Come on – take a bite from my life. How hard can it be?'

His smile faded and he stood. 'Silo – gimme a dumb gun.' Silencer handed him a Combat Magnum and Thermidor shot the chef in the eye. As he went over backwards Thermidor handed the gun back. 'Cause and effect, Neck. How great is that? Aluminium, lead shot, wads, some smoke. Keep your spirit levellers, you and your gumshoe. Yeah, Neck's got a gun with side impact bars, Atom, you and him got stuff in common. You want fries with that?' he shouted at the body, and sat down heavily at the table. 'Put him in the fire with the ants. Guess there's a lesson there for all of us. Sorry for the interruption, Atom. My life is complicated since my predecessor – whose memory I respect – died of bullet inhalation.' He drew the plate toward him and began eating again. 'Used to be Dino Korova's driver, way back. I'm tellin' ya hell's a roadmap with the lower half staining scarlet. My ma had to bust me out three times – people think Billy Panacea invented that scam, it was me.' He jabbed at his own chest with a fork. 'Now even my bodyguards got bodyguards, know what I mean? But still I have to deal with folk who run nuthin' but a temperature in this town. Folk like splatterpunk there. And folk like you.'

'Nobody's holdin' a gun to your beak.'

'Who else is gonna head this burg? Blince? Betty Criterion? One o' them three-day mayors? Who commands the fear round here but me? My own hairline's backdown scared, gumshoe.'

'I can tell your boy Fiasco's real respectful.'

'Fiasco.' Thermidor dabbed at his mouth with a napkin. 'He sleepwalked through a few bankjobs. An okay pelter, you know? Peach of a hairstyle. But young enough to think you need to go purchase trouble – don't know it's a charity. You know when Roni Loveless took the flight that time? Slap in the face for Korova but the boss was a patient man. Loveless was a hero in clench, until Korova seeded a rumour that the boxer had a fondness for mini veggies. That fall down the stairs was no accident. My point is, guilt's a debt in the head. I'll get my due from Harry Fiasco. And that's where you sweep in, Atom – but wasn't it yesterday I invited you into my life? What kept you?'

'Woke up thinking there was a bat in my room – something flapping round. Turned out to be the flying logo off a TV network – lost its bearings on the way to the station. Opened the window and tried to belt the thing out with a broom. But it was dumb, didn't understand I was trying to help. Kept on zooming and flapping, zooming and flapping. Finally slapped on to my ass and stuck.' He twisted around to show the logo on the cheek of his pants. 'Channel 10,000. Never watch it.'

'Just a regular guy, eh? Not what I heard. Eh, Neck? Our guest here's a real hard mark, right?'

Since Thermidor's talk of Atom's gun stance, Nada Neck had been taking the measure of the man. 'Seems kinda simple,' he muttered suspiciously.

'Kill-simple,' Thermidor smiled. 'Sure. Guy who ducks the story, ain't involved, punished by nuthin' but the lash of his own baby blues – that what we meant to think, wiseguy?'

'Almost that simple, Mr Thermidor. You know my father always told me, "If not for the light, how could we appreciate the darkness?" I guess in a town like this, recidivists and all, that man was an oddity – instead of committing the same badly thought-out offence over and over, he repeated the same crime a million times in his mind and only once in the flesh, a heist ending in his mournful death. His ghost continued to perform the raid every night, that unnatural forbearance in life having left his soul a million urges to vent. Some sour evenings, if you listen close, you can still hear Father trying to open that solid vault with transparent hands.'

In the storeroom, Minuteman was trying on Atom's coat. It fitted like a glove and made him feel fizzy inside. He realised it was closing up like a Venus flytrap. His vision started to spot and blur. He wasn't what you'd call satisfied, but couldn't breathe or complain. Bones bust with a dull thump. Pretty soon the coat went like a tube of toothpaste squeezed in a fist – pulped mobster erupted from both ends.

'Where's the squasher?' Thermidor was saying in the main hall.

Radiant with indifference, Atom gapped a yawn.

'Hey, mystery guest – I keepin' you up?'

'Barely.'

Thermidor picked up the phone and slammed it forward on the table. 'You get on the tumbler and bring it in or weird-and-gilly gets a headful of air.'

Atom strolled over and picked up the receiver, dialling.

'I figured you for a squirtgun,' smiled Thermidor in satisfaction.

'Do you believe in the transmigration of souls, Mr Thermidor?'

'Eh? No.'

'Then I'll thank you to keep your opinions to yourself. Maddy?' His attention turned to the phone. 'It's Taff. I need that item brought over to the mob's sandbox. Uh? Yeah, like we thought. Uh? Just pants, shirt, boots, leather waistcoat. No, they took the coat. The pants? Black. The logo, yeah. No, no underwear. I know it's cold. Right now? Cover you with jam. Okay. See you soon.' He replaced the phone. 'All set, Mr Thermidor.'

'Neck – bring the fish.'

'It's in the hot tub with Cherry and Linda, boss.'

'So interrupt it.'

As Nada Neck left, Atom sat down and swung his legs on to the table. 'Jed can entertain us while we're waiting for my associate.'

'Entertain us? How?'

'By pursing his lips like a fish.'

'He *is* a fish.'

'So why'd you seem surprised?'

Jed Helms' tank was rolled in on a drinks trolley. 'Hey Atom,' he burbled, 'I've had a taste o' Thermidor's life and I like it.'

'I'm here to rescue you Jed.'

'Rescue me? You gotta be kiddin.'

'You're suffering from Stockholm Syndrome, Jed. Transference – these people ain't your friends. Did they once tell you to shout a little louder?'

'Never had to.'

'I can believe it. Look at you, you're overheated.'

'I love it.'

Atom had meant for Jed to whistle 'Mack the Knife' during the interlude but the argument lasted the full eight minutes it took for Madison to arrive and the time passed pleasantly enough. Calm as the dead, Madison entered with a tin soccer ball and placed it on the table.

'Well, well – smoke and class. That one o' them cryo buckets? Hope the folds iron out, missy.' Thermidor laughed until his flunkeys caught on and added their contribution.

'He doesn't look like much,' said Madison to Atom, and the room fell abruptly silent.

'We'll just take the barracuda and be on our way, Mr Thermidor.'

But standing behind Atom and Drowner was a new arrival in a Luger suit.

Thermidor smiled, without astonishment. 'The prodigal stooge,' he said as Harry Fiasco approached the table. 'Here you walk right back into my life. Just in time for brunch and its bloody aftermath. Harry Harry Harry, you been busier than a fly tryin' to cover its eyes. Silo.' Silencer handed Thermidor the .357 and Thermidor raised it at Fiasco. As he clicked back the hammer it sounded like a skeleton's step in a cathedral. A ketchup tear trailed from his vegetable retina. 'Tell me it ain't so, Harry, that you boosted some valuable squasher and let it fall into the hands o' this shamus.'

'That's a sixpack o' lies, Mr Thermidor,' shouted Fiasco. 'Sure I boosted a brain but I did it for you, it's safe Mr Thermidor I swear.'

'I happen to have different information,' rumbled Thermidor, gunning his ego. Murky motivations clashed in the air like stormfronts.

'Like the hair, Harry,' Atom remarked. 'Got its own passport?'

'The gumshoe says the brain's in here.' Thermidor flicked the gun toward the metal orb.

'Sure and there's bees in the TV,' Fiasco scoffed. 'Take a look, you don't believe me.'

'A man with a gun is in no need of advice, boy,' stated Thermidor. He was trembling. 'I'll make you bleed till you can't stand the colour clash.'

'The hick's right, Mr Thermidor,' said Jed Helms.

'Lemme speak, I'm in the eye of an emotional hurricane here!' roared Thermidor, blasting the fishtank, which shattered down around Jed as he hunched like a kraken on a medieval map. 'Outta my way!' Thermidor fired the deafening Combat again as he approached the orb. 'I'm upset. Real upset. The goddamn squasher's in here you'll be ploughed up in twenty years, Fiasco. If it ain't, you Atom, and maybe you too Fiasco, and maybe every goddamn timewastin' sonofabitch here, are gonna wind up in a sluiceroom!' He grasped the orb and twisted its halves – the seam clicked. Everything went low res.

Like most flux technology, the Syndication bomb hinged on a cheap but ingenious trick. Rather than actually stripping the subtext from the blast site it converted the wave range into a living Updike novel, the subtext containing information everyone already knew – the end result was a shallow reality in which every move was a statement of the obvious. A bullet dopplered past Atom's ear but it didn't tell him anything fresh. Thermidor was going berserk, scaring his boys into drab chaos. All etheric firearms were neutralised by the flat bomb. Atom grabbed Jed and followed Madison out of the chamber. His coat burst from a storeroom like a bat out of hell and attached itself to him as though magnetised. In the car they slammed Jed into a portable circuit cooler and drove off a minute before the cops arrived, cherry lights whirling. No one was any the wiser.

*

Shiv waited on the corner of Amp as Kitty walked down Sunday. She'd been to the cop den so he'd had to hold off, but his blade already sang with anticipation.

As Kitty neared the alley mouth Shiv felt heat in his throat, and as she passed he was pulled back into the gloom. An angular, origami figure covered in coat had looped his neck with a wire. 'You're choking me.'

'Is it that obvious?'

Dr DeCrow, eyes distant as a fishgutter's, pulled at the snare. Shiv bent sideways like an awkward drunk, supporting himself awhile as though unaware he was dead.

'The young are too intent to be truly sinister.'

'Here's to plain speaking,' said the Candyman, raising a .38 snub in his chubby hand. 'And I'll have you know better than I, sir, wherever this bullet goes, the Geneva Convention is void. Come in and shut the door.'

Atom and Drowner closed the office door behind them.

Joanna was stood next to the Candyman with a chicaned H&K Terraform Cannon. The flared chrome barrel looked like the silencer off a race hog. Turow was stood against the blinds toying with a silver-handled cane.

'You sure the cracker can hold that pocket-edition howitzer without firing at memories of his ma? Room this size we'll be six feet under.'

'What's life without hazard?'

'Pleasant.'

'You're a man of nice judgement sir. There's more sense in the antler of a snail than in Joanna's entire frame. More than once it has been necessary to pay him with food meant for dogs. Eh, Joanna? But have you considered, Mr Atom, how his somewhat uncoordinated coercion would feel in circumstances of hurried duress?'

'It has crossed my mind – on skis, as a matter of fact.'

55

'Ah that's wonderful, sir, wonderful. But now I must ask Miss Drowner to step forward and place the brain in my trust.'

'Your truss?'

'My trust, Mr Atom.'

'Whatever,' muttered Madison, walking over with a languid precision and putting the circuit-coolant icebox on the desk. Turow moved forward, eyes bulbing.

'Keep them covered, Joanna.' The Candyman placed the Smith & Wesson aside and approached the icebox. 'And now, Mr Turow,' he said huskily, 'after seventeen years!' He popped the seal, licked his liver lips, and lifted the lid.

Two minutes later they stood in the street gasping with exertion, clothes torn, faces laminated with sweat. Trembling, Joanna curled down a wall on to a doorstep, where he lay like an abandoned newborn. 'I told you so!' rasped Turow. 'Dealing with Atom is like stepping off a mountain edge!'

'Take heart, Mr Turow. We are merely flogging a horse of a different colour.'

'You!' Turow spat in spluttering petulance, face flushed. 'It's you who bungled it! You and your hiring of Fiasco! He realised how valuable it was! You and your crunchy intrigues will have us tugging udders in Kansas, you – you dunderhead, you – imbecile, you – fat, bloated idiot, you . . .' And he broke off, blubbering, hands to his face, and turned against the wall.

The Candyman's jaw sagged. He blinked vacant eyes.

Then he shook himself, tuning back in. And once again he was jovial, his smile a cherub's.

'Well. I should never have doubted you, Turow. Everybody errs at times, and you may be sure this is as much a blow to me as to your good self. But what do you suggest? That we stand here shedding tears and yelling abuse, or redouble our efforts?'

Turow took his hands from his face but gave him no reply.

'Regrettably it seems Atom is of such a calibre our negotiations must of necessity be less diplomatic, and irreversible. Something further may follow of this masquerade.'

9

Napoleon in the Desert

'Fiasco!'

There was no getting past it – Henry Blince was a cop as far as the eye could see. Once he had almost been persuaded to sell advertising space on his butt, a near lapse he chose not to remember. Smoking a cigar which seemed to have been carved from an expensive chair, he looked up at the gang fort and considered which rendition of the evidence would prove most damaging for the kid. The more he speculated the more proof he made.

'You're bound for the hotseat, Fiasco,' he yelled through the hailer. 'It's funny because it's true, sparky. Come on down.'

'Think he'll surrender, Chief?' asked Benny the Trooper, squinting up at Blince.

'If there's any justice, Benny. Fiasco's breathin' in breach o' the law.'

'Killin' people and like that, right, Chief?'

'Bet your sweet life and nobody forced him. One time Fiasco did an installation job wearin' a jacket made o' parachute silk. Used a mime as a human shield. Made for a better flailing pattern when the bullets hit. Weren't you there, Benny?'

'Vacation, Chief. Hawaii.'

'That where the locals gave you a wreath in advance? Ain't that a welcome.'

'Give 'em to everyone, Chief. They're a pessimistic culture. Invented surfing.'

'Hey speakin' o' which, do fish ever get the bends, Benny? It's been naggin' and naggin' at my troubled mind – I mean when you consider some live at such depths they ain't got any pigmentation.'

'I guess some o' them transparent puffers might burst, Chief,' Benny muttered uncertainly, looking off, 'ascend fast enough.'

'Well you're a regular suppository o' wisdom, Benny, lemme ask you somethin' else. If we had to hit this premises full on, would you enter by the gate or the roof?'

'I ain't too keen to hit the mob with this triage ammo, Chief.' Benny had just been issued with an Ithaca intel with no more recoil than an arcade gun.

'You'll shoot it and like it, trooper boy. The shinin' truth is, Thermidor ain't likely to give up his goon. Got some kinda code, a choice blend o' fact and fiction. Made his bones with Korova by machine-gunnin' four hundred Elvis impersonators from a municipal tower. Shots and slurred obscenities. Rex Camp was just startin' out as the Coroner and he had his hands full. Excess o' hair gel caused an explosion in the furnace. That shootin' and the attendant emotional baggage earned everyone's respect. While we stand here booted and shootered, Thermidor's probably laughin' in the light of an orgy lamp.'

'So why we here, Chief?'

'Cause we're cops, Benny. Sittin' pretty in the carbon cycle. And it keeps the red wings of our hearts a-flappin'.'

'There's Fiasco, Chief.'

A crack in the armoured gate boomed shut behind Harry Fiasco as he walked forward with his hands raised.

'You're under arrest for scatterin' brains across the public highway like crabs headin' for the spawnin' beach,' stated Blince as he drew near. 'You've achieved a capital crime.'

'Thank you, Mr Blince.'

'Read him his whatsername rights, Benny.'

'"Miranda", Chief.'

'What you call yourself off-duty's a matter for a higher authority than mine, trooper boy.'

ATOM'S JOURNAL

I can't help thinking about bleak-featured panthers, hamsters with puffy cheeks, loggerhead turtles rocking on the ocean. A sad subway captain, tentacles furred like thistles. A cat – the kind that looks like a cigar's exploded in its face. A city father knocked incredulous in a storm drain. Bees can't hear, but they seem to know when to scramble.

Turow was coming apart like a soaked loaf. Walking up Valentine in pants with a street value of five dollars, he was taken back to another street in Tangier, which he'd trodden in those same pants. A merchant had even attempted to sell him a dress and an argument had ensued in the course of which the merchant, though struggling through a foreign language, had made it explicitly clear that Turow did not possess enough guts to stink in death. Turow had been gasping with indignation when the Candyman made his first appearance.

'I couldn't help but overhear your dispute with this scoundrel, sir. Only an irredeemable opportunist would attempt to sell a dress to a man of your obvious integrity.'

'What do you know about it?'

'A great deal, sir, and I mean that in every possible sense.

Objects of true and lasting value go often undetected among these marketeers – unless rescued by the likes of you and I. Candyman's the name, sir, and I'll have you know better than I do I admire a man sir who knows how to talk about admiring a man who admires a man who admires a man . . .'

The memory burbled into nonsense as Turow entered the Delayed Reaction Bar. He was thirsting for clarity – for fixity of purpose.

'What's it gonna be then?' asked the barman. 'White-coat? Yellowbird? Mighty Wurlitzer?'

'Do you know how to make a Treadmill Existence?'

'Sure. Eats? Look like you're on your last knees.'

Turow regarded a steaming plate on the bartop bearing a large crustacean of perhaps extraterrestrial origin – the pungency rising from it fogged all hope of a dialogue. Turow brought a scented kerchief to his mouth. 'If you'll pardon me for saying so, this particular dish raises more questions than it answers.'

'I call that "Schulz's Last Escape". Hey, which reminds me, hear the news? Fiasco fries with the fishes.'

'What?' said Turow, as though slowly awaking.

'Fiasco's bein' measured for an urn. UnAmerican pro-clivities.'

Turow was querulous. 'When did this happen?'

'Just heard.' Toto started the blender. 'Ten million stories in the armoured city. Weren't you in here the other day askin' Flea about Fiasco?'

'Atom!' Turow whispered emphatically. 'That sick time-waster will have me siphoning fuel in sub-zero temperatures.' And he placed his face upon the bartop until a pool of tears had darkened the surface.

'Yeah, the Atman's a dark horse,' Toto continued, ob-livious as he cleaned a glass. 'PI modality. Father used to be the cook at the mayor's fort uptown. Even at that time the mayor was not brimming with the spice, I'll tell ya. If he had a self-renewing penny he'd spend it at the barber's. Any bastard here has more imagination in his lapels than the moron I'm describing. Public deplored him and moved on from broad hints to blazing gunfire. Atom's old man was one of the mayor's most side-on enemies. Young man then of course. Back-thwacking popularity. Soul rare as a double coconut. Ethics and edgy fortitude. Youth in the modern style. Felt a thousand years tired rather than a thousand years wise – constant pain alters a man's priorities, as you'll know. And what dumbfounded him most was that the office of mayor seemed always to be snagged by a fool resembling a drumfish in a big scarf, you know? So he decided to kill the mayor and take his place. I know some of the fraudulent generalities required, he thought. All I need is a clean shirt and a set of eyes which close without appearing to.'

Way behind Turow the bar's darkness shifted like an orchestra pit of giant insects.

'Transparent lids,' muttered someone. 'Like an owl.'

'I guess, Hammy. So the cook knew he'd be suspected if he poisoned the mayor and therefore decided to shove him off the balcony during a speech. The mayor had the sense to realise he was in danger but lacked the rich imagination to avert it, choosing his duty over his rights. And we all know the difference between a right and a duty.'

'You certainly don't expect me to comment,' said Turow from the crash position.

'A right is something we want to do and for which we receive no thanks,' continued the barman, 'while a duty is something we don't want to do and for which we receive no thanks. The mayor went out to gurn at the masses and, as one does on these occasions, the cook pushed the drab official into the crowd, where he was crushed like a walnut in a franking machine. The cook was elected to mayor and hailed the heavens with his laughter.'

Don Toto stopped cleaning the glass a moment, frowning into the middle distance, then continued.

'However, the townspeople began to blather about a weird scuttling creature they were glimpsing and Atom's pa – now the mayor – suffered a gnarly fear. Putting together certain facts he realised that just before the murder, the mayor had burnt an advance denunciation of the cook into the carapace of a landcrab which the cook had left fully alive on a platter, like how the French leave lobsters lying around the place sniggering and so on for hours before toasting them, you know. The mayor had then set it loose.'

'Excuse me, did I hear you correctly?' Turow said drowsily, looking up with dawning and tortured amazement. 'You say that certain facts led him to think all this? A landcrab? Which facts led him, or I might add you, to believe this fable?'

'Not least the mayor's bellowed remark to the cook that he knew he was trying to poison him, the mayor's subsequent meddling with a butane torch, and the fact that the crab was missing after the murder. In fact probably the mayor believed the crab itself contained poison and would therefore provide proof positive when it was captured.'

'But of course. How could I have been so foolish?'

'So there was a giant landcrab skittering through the black alleys,' Toto resumed, 'scrawled with damning evidence. Thoughts of the beast haunted the new mayor's every instant. Okay so finally he went mad, the pleasure of which was so intense that everyone remarked upon his improved spirits. To escape the anticipated trial he resolved to oblong himself, so that when the crustacean

64

was finally snared, his own death would be blamed on the new cook, a guy of whom he was rightly suspicious. In the event the new cook ventilated him anyway and made it appear to be suicide, taking his place as mayor.'

'Unless I am sadly mistaken, the hero of your story is now dead.' Turow fumbled in his jacket for a cigarette.

'By now rumours were circulating that the alley crab had some profound message on its back, okay? But even in those days the cops avoided anything likely to imperil their ignorance. The beast was bigger than ever, and at people's approach it'd rear up, brandishing fully its serrated claws. Despite the creature's habit of scuttling sideways the curious few were bent on a head-on confrontation and so the message on its back remained unseen by those to whom it would mean a damn. The truth's generally left alone – like the samurai-faced crabs of the Inland Sea which fishermen throw back for fear of bad luck, the descendants of this one, scrawled with the truth, inherited the shell-pattern through natural selection and bear it to this day.'

There was a static-filled silence. 'I beg your pardon?' Turow said at last, the Egyptian cigarette dangling dead from the dry lower lip of his gob. 'Have you perhaps misplaced your reason? "Inherited the shell-pattern"?'

'Reality evades the eye,' said the barman, holding a clean glass to the light, 'dodging the rods and cones like a swerve driver.'

'Keeps to the eye corners,' muttered someone way back in the bar's gloom, 'where there's no colour perception.'

'Truth ain't black and white either, Hammy.'

'So what is it, in your opinion?' asked Turow.

'The colour of a diamond.'

'Well it has certainly been a pleasure,' said Turow, standing down from his stool. 'Thank you for your attempts to cheer me in my dark hour. But I must say I wish you would have invented a more reasonable story. Good day to you.'

'Light?' said the barman mildly, producing a Zippo.

Turow took the cigarette from his mouth as though surprised to find it there, then replaced it and leaned over – the barman sparked the flint and the crustacean reared from the platter of veggies nearby, clacking its claws. Reflected in every glass in the bar, the slogan THE COOK KILLED ME was etched in its shell. Screaming like the damned, Turow whacked the barman's arm aside and the crab burst into flames, launching itself from the bartop and emitting a semisonic scream as it skittered flaring across the floor to collide with a gun-stand. The stand ignited and the bar erupted into panic as a dozen guzzlers paid off at once. Turow was out the door like a rabbit out of a trap. 'Spray your vehicle,' said the barman, 'it's still the old colour underneath.'

10

Mutant Jazz

Madison's windshield TV superimposed the spectacle over the traffic. 'News on the hour. The President, whose assassination is said to be at a delicate stage, has described his hourly bare-knuckle efforts to "stay clean" after being discovered *in flagrante* with a four-foot squid. The squid is a carnivorous marine mollusc with a streamlined body and shell reduced to an internal cartilaginous rod. "My enemies would love to use this regrettable impulse against me. I believe this says more about their sickness than mine." Tomorrow's Presidential visit to Beerlight City amid the continuing breakup of states is widely viewed as a carnage opportunity.

'Mobster Harry Fiasco has been convicted of psychological damage and condemned to the chair on the three strikes longcon after destroying the City Brain Facility. "I'd like to thank my mom, my dad, my girlfriend Kitty, my parole officer and all the victims who made this possible. This execution's for you." But the execution has been postponed for the purpose of publicity. On the steps of the court Attorney Harpoon Specter commented, "You'll notice I'm grimacing. All the muscles in my face have contracted due to the terrific velocity of these proceedings. Indeed the trial was so swift I had very little airtime. I aim to stay this execution for at least sixteen hours. Beauty surrounds me. Outta my way." When asked why he turned Fiasco in, mob boss Eddie Thermidor was evasive. "Didn't seem significant at the time." '

'And in response to the production of Dead Barbie, a grey doll with no eyes, parents have complained that the product is otherwise indistinguishable from other Barbies. Manufacturers were adamant. "The notion that we're simply saving paint is nonsense. We want to instruct kids about mortality. The new Barbie has a casket, cadaver makeup, bugs. Alive she is not." That was the news and bother – this is the number one video – "What's With the Knife" by Septal Erosion.'

Madison drew up at the state pen. Fiasco had been sentenced in a court resembling a third-world bazaar. As the jury entered they were garrotted by the rigging. 'Correct the offender forever,' the judge told them, 'or the impulse to imitate will overwhelm.' It was hard to tell which side Harpoon Specter was on. 'Nothing could be said about Harry Fiasco which has not been said before,' he declared. 'Feisty in every department of life, he has stamped his personality on my face and those of many gathered here. He's so brave his balls are a threat to us all.' Auto-Rhino's explosive termination a few years back had put an end to the killing jar – Harry was headed for the Rosenberg rocker.

Beyond the glass of the gawpers' room was a chamber side-slapped with migraine bars. Fiasco was brought over all decked out in electrolock manacles and dropped opposite. Despite the pen gear, the flip-up contacts and bulletproof tan made him an easy mark for a fashion prefab. He frowned at the visitor – there were raindrops on her coatcollar, on the brim of her hat. 'Told me I had a visit I thought it was Kitty. Where'd I see you before?'

'You know Taffy Atom to say hell to, Harry? You saw us at the Fort. I'm his partner.'

'Atom. PI modality, right? And there was some story 'bout his daddy.'

'Head clown at the circus. Killed in a miniature car pile-up. Went right over the hood. All four wheels came off. Taff never got over it.'

'Tough break. So you're Drowner. Say, how do I look?'

'Underdone. But you're gonna look like a dorito, honey.'

'Dead-on balls accurate.'

'So the end won't be tepid.'

'My style. You know me and Kitty used to have taser sex.'

'She doesn't say much for you.'

'She's a reserved lady.'

'So much so,' Madison put a shock absorber between her lips and lit it, 'she ain't there.'

'No recoil on a remote – she's the perfect crime.'

'Nobody's perfect, Harry. You shoulda left town when you had the chance.'

'My ethics were in development hell. I never done nuthin' like that before.'

'Like what.'

'Goin' freelance. I figured someday me and Kitty'd be livin' in a twenty-mile house havin' foodfights with beluga, you know? What, I meant to stay at that job till I put my fist through it? Easy as fallin' in line, sure. But when I took a swatch at that squasher . . .'

'You knew it had to be valuable, right? The gent went to that much trouble.'

'Not right off.' Fiasco looked abashed. 'Guess I consider alertness a sorta insecurity. Delivered the brain to the Candyman, but after, I started gettin' like an intuition. Some feel a twinge in the leg with a change o' weather – I feel it in my shirt. Get a real anchor in my pants. So I go back the next day and boost the brain, take a good blink at that baby. Looks like a tree disease and feels like a soft-boiled egg. Then I realise, I don't know where to sell a squasher. Don't even know why it's such a big deal. By now I got a head o' steam worked up. I can't fence it, can't go back to the gent, so I figure maybe I pitch it to Thermidor, tell him I happen to see a good thing and pursue it like on his behalf, nobody's any the wiser as usual. But by now a little time's passed, I don't know what reception I'll get, if I'll have to run for it, so of course I don't swan into the Fort with the goods up front. The easiest way to lose your mind's to mail it.'

'Deposit box?'

'Beerlight Grand. Five-eight-nine. Mailed the key to Santa Claus.'

'Funny.'

'What?'

'Why you spilling this, Harry? Me and Taff haven't exactly helped you.'

'Something's turned around, Miss Drowner. That death sentence was like a declaration of love, you know? A few words and the whole world changed. Life kicked me hello.'

'You get free, the mob'll take you to pieces and lose the manual.'

'I ain't gettin' out, miss – Blince stores resentment in his cheeks like a hamster. Guess I'll pop like a bug on a hotplate, yeah.'

Madison stubbed the shock. 'Well, it's been good, Harry.' She stood to go.

'Hey miss, you see Kitty you tell her I love her. Tell her I'll be waitin' on the dry side.'

'Sure, Harry.'

70

Madison started down the passage away from the gawping room.

'Life shoots first, lady,' Fiasco shouted after her.

As she neared the end of the passage, Henry Blince turned the corner coming the other way. 'Well looky here. How long you know Scatterbrains, Miss Drowner?'

'How long you been walking erect?'

'Aw come on Maddy, you're breakin' my heart here.'

'Break your own heart – I'm busy.'

She strode on, leaving him stunned with respect.

Nada Neck dropped by the hospital acting breezy. 'Lookin' good, Flea. Love the ears. Wanted to apologise for shootin' you in the bar.'

'Ah forget it.' Flea kept eating a melon as Neck strolled past the bed to the window. 'In fact you did me a favour. Seems I committed a crime that day – a new one. Caere Twins are in here to make a bleak assessment.'

'Heard this place is goin' down for some three strikes landfill. Yeah, postage stamps'll have skulls on 'em in this town. Which reminds me.' Walking over, he dug from his pocket a drift of confetti bearing Atom's likeness, and snowed it on to Flea's bed. 'I don't know if this is gold dust or a swatted moth. Want to fill me in?'

'I filled you in,' said Flea, up and voluble. 'Damn straight.'

'Flea on the wall, eh? How's your chest?'

'I'm on top of the weather.' Flea put down a melon segment and wiped his hands on the sheet. 'Okay. I once seen Atom dead-lift the end of a '69 Volkswagen Bug. He pulled his right shoulder and broke his back in three places. Quite a guy. Said he thought a chicken was a dove on stilts.'

'We only got wit in this city to fool our mothers, Flea. You called Atom a shadowman.'

'Yeah. Low key. Got a dog that's inside-out. Uses its windpipe as a leash. Tells people he's a house painter. Entered the Reaction once with a charming spear.'

'How can a spear be charming?'

'By deceit.'

'So he's untrustworthy.'

'I didn't say that.'

'Flea.' Neck lit a shock. 'I'm a busy guy.'

'Well okay. Okay, how can I put this? Let's say he's the sort who'd mail his appendix to a starving man.'

'So what. Nobody cares about that part.'

'He does. He loves it.'

'He loves his appendix.'

'That's what I said. He kisses it all the time.'

Neck took an irritable pull at the gasper. 'How can a man kiss his own appendix?'

'He'll do all kinds of things if you let him.'

'Well, don't. Not if he's taking those sorta chances. God almighty.'

'Atom's wounds run deep, Neck. You know that experiment where they give different drugs to spiders and see what kinda webs they weave? Speed makes a wreck, burgers make the ancient smiley and so on? Atom's old man was an architect. Got bit by a tarantula. Started creating arthropodal buildings – octopolar, eight points to 'em, right? Tarantula venom's a cerebro-spinal stimulant, alters the mind, used in gypsy brews to release what they call the "dark burning soul". Permanently imprints the nervous system, so it's not just a quest drug. These buildings were extradimensional – deep wings, open corners, corridors in impossible directions. The old man called the blueprints treasure maps. One day when Taff was a kid his pa disappeared in one o' them structures. Taff went into the study to get the blueprint – it was stuck flat on the wall, and floating in the air in the middle of the room was one o' them crosses that mark the spot, already fading. By the time he'd called someone to look, it was gone. And he never saw his pa again.'

In silence a while, Neck gave unfazed by scrutinising his cigarette, then appeared to remember Flea. 'Flea, I hate to be one o' those people, but . . .'

'I know how it sounds, Nada, believe me. You know the weird strip off Scanner, used to be Fall Street? Now there's just a squirly dark, sorta makes you dizzy to go near? Atom discharged a gun there, gun to conjure with called a Glory Hand.'

'Some kinda smart flaw?'

'Suck gun. I hear it really wails.'

'An etheric?'

'Ethigraph gridpulse and all, what I heard, samples the victim's deal and flips it, like them martial arts that dodge your thrust and carry you down with your own weight, you know? Enough venom in a scorpion to kill a scorpion.'

'So he uses the enemy.'

'This is Beerlight, Neck – situationism's just a front.'

Neck had sucked the gasper to a stub. 'First shock of the day's the most intense.' He flicked it away.

'Hello, blabber,' called the Caere Twins brightly, sticking their heads round the door. They came in different as twilight and twilight and beamed at Nada Neck. 'Hello, straight-up.'

'I was just leaving.' Neck sauntered to the door. 'Swat you later, Roach.'

When Neck was gone, the Twins sat on either edge of Flea's bed. Their silence made him apprehensive. 'It's bad, isn't it?'

'We don't know how to tell you, Flea.'

'What you drivin' at?'

73

'When beaker let rip with that M61 Persuader,' said a Twin gently, 'it forced an etheric sample of his intent to kill you, into the charm filter's etheric bromide shield.'

'We thought,' the other Twin continued, 'that the overlap of the two may have synthesised something new.'

'Like what?'

'A residue from the neutralised intent. Created between you at the raw level. It wasn't a mere deflection because it affected base particles of Nada's etheric.'

'So break it to me, what's the charge?'

'Oh, poor Flea. It could have been "the infringement of another's will at the soul source". This would go beyond the known taxonomy of offence.'

'But?'

'Only the etheric fired at you was negated. Nada retained plenty within him.'

'So? I went with intent to commit.'

'No, Flea. You didn't really know what the bib was – your manoeuvre was inadvertent. I'm so sorry.'

'This can't be right. I . . . I drew the gunfire by being the target – metaphysical provocation, right? Inciting violence.'

'Take care of yourself, Mr Lonza,' said the Twins, standing.

'Wait, there's laws on incitement, nuthin on this soul bullshit.' Flea was frantic. 'Don't legislation qualify somethin' for a crime?'

'Oh no, Mr Lonza,' they said. 'Everyone knows what's a *real* crime.'

'I even commit an offence on paper?'

The Twins stopped at the door, looking back at Flea with profoundest pity. 'Goodbye, flyboy.'

Alone, Flea gibbered. 'I didn't do *anythin'* wrong?'

Walking down the corridor, the Twins stopped short, turning to one another big-eyed.

'The infringement of another's will at the soul source,' whispered one.

'Legislation,' gasped the other.

With the advent of polymer flesh lacing a few years later the Twins would start souping up geneware to develop perplex, simple organic matter which could be programmed directly from whichever personality profile the cops favoured for a particular offence. Nearly a thousand red herringbone diversion puppets were set loose across the eastern seaboard to attract arrest. Only nineteen perps fulfilled their destiny, going to the chair without a thought in their fungal heads – the rest sat moulding in rented rooms or became tenured professors.

11

The Gat Man

The Fort was pure Hatland but Neck needed more than patter and dumbguns to be a good right arm. He opened his walk-in arsenal and took a swatch. The chamber glinted black like a nest of spiders. It had the parliamentary vibe of dead energy. Armbone's connected to the handbone, handbone's connected to the triage Starflare Street Sweeper semi-auto twelve-round with eighteen-inch barrel and three-second void. Guns for all occasions – mood guns, metabolics, vogues, voyeurs, fuzzies, carnatics, geodesics, diagnostics. A Lusa Palmtop. A Tantrum gun. A Penrose rifle, automatic as mother nature. A roid rod – bad gun, he'd hallucinated behind it. A squidgrenade resembling a sea urchin. A tetanus missile. A Liberty Bell. Calico seeds. Murex ammo. A gun of blown glass which evaporated when fired once. Cryo ice bullets. A patented eyelash hammer. Steak throwknives. And here, an Eschaton rifle with a gull-wing chamber and fruitwood inlay grip. Draw a bead and speed the victim to his cosmic conclusion, be it ashes or glory. Metaphysical roulette, loaded to the ashes. Its designer, Johnny Pilot Fish, had theorised that the weight of the soul was the difference between a person's weight before death and after. To determine this he had to know when certain deaths were going to occur and got on the grapevine with the city shooters – it got so that when

Johnny turned up to weigh someone, they knew they were about to get hit. Johnny was baffled when he found that the victims weighed the same before and after. It was Rex Camp the Coroner who pointed out that the victim's body now included a bullet. Johnny PF's Equaliser Theory – how the soul weighs the same as the bullet that evicts it – was born to please its parents. But as everyone's favourite gun guru Brute Parker said, a theory's only as good as the speed it can leave a Weatherby Mark V.

'Well,' said Neck, 'these bullets ain't gonna fire theirselves.' It would be six years before the first gun became fully sentient. He hefted the Eschaton, breathing hard in the dumb air.

'There's no such thing as a normal angel,' Atom whispered, looking down at the city. 'It's never done that way.'

Madison stuck her head out the window, smoking a cigarette. 'Don't do this to me, Taff. We need to talk.'

Atom crawled along the ledge and climbed into the office. 'How was Fiasco – boastful and disappointing as a hacker?'

'Don't be such a heel. Fiasco's kinda honest. Confused and outside the dollars, he just grabbed like a monkey.'

'Sounds dumb.'

'Great things can sound dumb. Anything sound more dumb and annoying than the hammering of a nail?'

'Nail in his own coffin?'

'Simmer down, Taff. Come to that, you and me are two sides of the same lid.'

Atom looked on with chuffed awe as she related the brain deal. Maddy was so deep he needed a U-boat to visit her.

'There's something strange about the gent, Taff,' she was

saying. The desk light flashed an intruder. 'He's been . . . modified.'

'Jackfitted?'

'No, but he's been worked on, I can feel it. Like he's out by remote control.'

'So who's at the switch – Harpo Marx?'

Turow slammed in looking all squeezed out. 'Atom! I've had more than I could ever hope to take!'

'I took you for an all-terrain toady, Turow. Capable o' drinkin' milk if you had to. Now you're claimin' to be small pyjamas?'

Turow appeared to be losing ground in his fight against insanity. He fiddled with a string of translucent plastic flakes.

'It'll be orange walls and shuffleboard, Turow. What you got there?'

'They used to be worry beads.' Turow shot a nervous glance at Madison, then shuffled up to Atom. 'I need to talk to you.'

'Go ahead.'

'Is there some other place?'

'Millions. That all you wanted to know?'

'What game is it you are playing?'

'You see my game every time you visit my office, Turow. Siddown.'

Turow sat in the client seat, and looked aside at the towering Madison.

'You're eighty per cent sebum, honey,' she said.

'Where is your sea monster?'

'Body shop,' said Atom, sitting opposite the desk.

'Thank goodness,' muttered Turow, wiping his brow with a silk kerchief. 'I must say it is most difficult to conduct one's affairs with that antisocial moray chewing the scenery.'

'Less distracting than a windchime.'

'What is that on the desk?'

'Just a raisin.'

'I thought it was a spider.'

'In your dreams.' Atom flicked the raisin into space.

'You despise me, don't you?'

'Lemme put it smartly, Mr Turow – I can't tell the difference between beef and your leg. You've been jerking like a puppet since day one.'

'You are a deeply disturbed individual,' Turow rasped strenuously, leaning forward.

'There's the cops, there's the mob, there's me – you gotta find your echelon.'

'Is that like a turtle?'

'Forget it, Taff,' said Maddy. 'You couldn't trust this guy to sit the right way on the john.'

'How dare you! I came here in good faith!'

'Packin' what?'

'Information, Mr Atom.' Turow's voice dropped to a hushed whisper. 'About the Candyman. He is a learned gentleman – has written a book proving this. But he is not interested in the man Kafka for scholarly purposes.'

'Funny-bone of the Gogol Schulz arm.'

'Perhaps – I bow to your knowledge, Mr Atom. But I must tell you the Candyman is fired with the unfashionable fear that we will all yet peel and split in a nuclear oven.'

'He's probably right,' said Atom, lighting a shock and leaning back.

'He says that only the sliding insects of the ground will survive the firestorm. And he has been positively growing tusks trying to create a breed of human insect which will continue to live on this accursed planet.'

'Everyone needs a goal.'

'You do not understand,' whined Turow, agitated. 'He has before placed the brain of a bug into a person, and the brain of a person into a bug. These horrors he has already accomplished.'

Atom had heard of this sort of thing. A guy called Kiddy Dasouza had felt he was a trout trapped in a man's body and saved for a trans-species operation. He blew the money on a greyhound and in desperation tried to download his head into Jed's body. But his mind was rejected for harbouring optimism. It seemed fish were machines, manmade or not.

'Guess the results were staple-eyed and rigid.'

'Quite rigid, Mr Atom. But now the Candyman intends to develop brains which are, shall we say, half and half.'

'You drop a little acid this morning, Turow?' asked Madison mildly.

'She's got a point there, Turow. Or shellfish. Hey wait a minute – you're saying the gent's some kinda brain surgeon?'

'No, Mr Atom – he employed a man, Dr DeCrow – I despise him. He carries with him strange devices, like a door-to-door dentist. He is the kind to keep his ancestors as ornaments. Even the Candyman began not to trust him – switched bases in fear of betrayal.'

'So the gent reckons the old roach brother's brain'll be a model for some bugman he wants to create.'

'It sounds farfetched, Mr Atom, but you have my assurance that this is the Candyman's fervent belief.'

'Well for what it's worth, Turow, we just found out where the squasher is.'

Turow goggled like a king prawn. 'You mean you never . . . You never had the brain in the first place!' He spluttered, gasping. 'I'll break off your arms and use them to paint the town, you . . . you . . .'

'You really have an attitude, you know that?' said Maddy, smiling at Atom with her whole body.

'Your body's a temple, babe, but your head's a cathedral.' Atom put on a pair of blacklight shades. 'I'll draw the gun out the core, then we go fork the noodle.'

Under Atom's brownstone was a catacomb maze based on a CAT scan of his cranium. Seeing the elevator descending, Neck had dashed down endless echoing stairs, then into passageways thrumming with hidden machinery, and was now worming down the crawlspace between two banks of piping. Hauling the Eschaton gun, he reached a metal grille – beyond was a sheer airshaft roaring with burnt dust.

Looking like a raven, Atom strode along a causeway projecting out across the well and ending in empty space. Here was a chrome display stand holding a firearm. It looked like a .38 slimline armani made of black diamond. Peering, Neck could believe it had no internal works at all, a fetish statuette. Its vented flank was like that of a stealth craft.

But when Atom touched it – just before everything blew to hell – the gun went clear as glass. Neck's dread really picked up. Then he was watching a trapdoor heaven of dislocating walls, monstrous laughter and bursting glare. Birth voices, faint blobs of landscape and blood butterflies tornadoed the air. Atom was a shadowed spectre under raining wounds and draining descent. Yellow spinelight poured down the wellshaft, flaring his shades and beating his coat. Starstreaks fell into deeps. Neck's senses began strobing. Glimpses of teeth throwing sparks. Red fingers embracing the gun grip. A city of glaring needles. Then he couldn't see anything, the orbits of his skull shocked cold.

Ghostburnt, he staggered into a street oiling with rain.

12

Whatever You Are Is Starting to Show

'I found the gent's beetle book on the dredge,' said Maddy as Atom ducked into the car. Turow was sat in back looking beleaguered. Maddy brought up a screen in the rainblurred windshield. 'It's called *Stag Mother, Look at Me.*'

Atom scrolled, reading as they peeled out.

'*An alert child could tell you that life shrinks like a low island. Organised religion added Jesus to the food groups. The past is killed off by American marksmen. The obligation to possess money, the forced flowers of convention, replicated controversy, canned gunfire, the ordeal venom of litigation, the dwindling comb-over of western culture – here, written in blood and English, is the hobbling of humanity. Mankind arms the threshold of inspiration lest it be taken by wit.*'

'We've got a tail,' said Atom.

'*Ambition shows on my watch. It is absurd to believe that nature attacks morality – likewise we are unfit to judge the scurrying creatures within our walls. They are alien to us, and so what is the measure of their greatness or their folly? Insects are not costumed. Trends neglect to illuminate them and their souls are not copied. They squirm and quiver for apparently excellent reasons. Their defences grow from within. As our own time passes, guilt is identical to progress. The heat death approaches and my dreams clatter with the ratcheting limbs of an arthropod.'*

'Getting dark. This the general tone?'

'Later it's devotional and supplicatory – there's a whole chapter on antennae. He calls them lovely whips.'

'They are,' Atom blurted. He screened his sudden embarrassment behind a makeshift expression of bright complacency. 'Er, here we go then, babe – Beerlight Grand.'

Maddy gave him a withering look and pulled in.

'Bring the denials?' asked Atom as they entered the station.

'Thought you had them.'

'How we both escape without allow cloaks?'

'I'm not in the mood anyway,' said Maddy. 'Here's the box.'

Atom popped the door with a one-use squidkey – inside was a regulated cryo cooler. Maddy slid it out and studied the console. 'Lotta system in here.'

Atom hit the release and steam burst out all over. He flipped the lid to glimpse a white mushroom of compact convolutions, and immediately slammed it. 'Here's not the place,' he decided. He closed the deposit box and broke off the hardgum key in the lock.

They strode across the concourse, Atom carrying the cooler by the handle.

After what he'd seen of Atom in that ventilation shaft, he couldn't risk concluding him with the Eschaton. So Neck had hit off the restraining pin on the Persuader semi, converting it to full-ego. His intent was cranked to the max.

Parked in the alley behind Beerlight Grand, he checked his gun by the light of the headlamps. A tin door banged and opened – he advanced upon it, rain dripping from the

Persuader muzzle. Atom emerged with a cooler case. A wedge of dark matter was leaking across his other hand.

'Last time I saw that, it looked like a glass gun. What's it made of?'

Staring down the barrel of Neck's flaw, Atom recovered fast. 'Carbon,' he said.

'Gimme the skull tackle, Atom.'

'In exchange for?'

'If you weren't so smart I'd give you some advice. But it's raining. And whatever you are is starting to show. Sorry this has to end inconveniently for you.'

When Nada Neck let rip, he was sucked into the rifle grip like a shrivelling balloon, bones powdering, and spurted from the muzzle as a volley of blood, pulp and water. The guzzler emptied and fibrillated. A pink cloud swirled before Atom. Then the gun fell from the air and clattered to earth.

Atom pulled Neck's car into Waits Street as Madison arrived from the opposite direction. Atom jumped cars and they screeched off. 'Still got that tail,' said Maddy.

'Who is it?' strained Turow.

'The Candyman. Behind that, Eddie Thermidor. Behind that, someone looking really ill.'

A sideparked patrol car sparked up and swerved after.

'And the dead.'

Madison had left Beerlight Grand with her coat bunched out and the waiting crew had taken it for the squasher. Now Atom popped the hamper and took a swatch. Soft clay sheened with cold sweat. Maddy glanced over. 'It looks strange, doesn't it?'

'We are followed by four automobiles and you are discussing—' Turow leaned forward and saw the brain, his rant cut short. His voice became hushed. 'Is that it?'

'That's the crap axis all right,' Atom muttered. He felt yellow waves wolfing out of the squasher and staining the air. 'Funeral sends us to the attic and we're forgotten, but not him. I'll bet this beauty weighs five pounds. You could use it for a sparring pad. Doesn't feel like I thought he would, though. The kirlian's like shit.'

They swerved into Singh with a harsh tearing of tyres. The headlights swept across brawls and graffiti.

'Wouldn't it be? He saw pretty clear. Just screaming on the wrong side of his face.'

'Depends on his defences, I guess.'

'Weren't the books his defence?' Madison asked as they entered the Portis Thruway.

'Art's an exploding sandwich.'

'Doesn't fail, then. But what if it's fake?'

'For a fake to be identified, a difference has to be detected, right? But if it's a different work, why's it classed a fake? Because some morons can't distinguish between one work and another?'

'Oh, you kid.'

The lights of the thruway streaking behind her, she blew him a kiss that unravelled his stitches.

'Why are we chasin' Dumpy, Mr Candyman? Why's he in the wiseguy's car?'

'You know, when I look at you, Joanna, I realise how far we've come as a species after all.'

Joanna turned back and gave him a sloppy grin.

'Fools will assure you they take no sides – wise men that they do. Both lie. Names are captive to record. Don't be captive to your name, my boy.'

'You want I should bean the car, Mr Candyman?'

'Use the Ingram – the snub's as useless as posthumous vindication. And a tad more speed, if you please.'

Joanna thought so slow he saw everything around him in

timelapse – to his mind they were travelling at four hundred miles an hour. He raised the M11 as slow as an hour hand and started blazing without opening a window – the windshield exploded outward.

'Hang on to your hat, Joanna,' shouted the Candyman above the scream of the thruway. 'To be shot, whoever does the shooting, is disagreeable.'

'Can't my life move any faster?' barked Thermidor from the back seat. At the wheel, Sam 'Sam' Bleaker didn't reply, but on Brute Parker's advice he regularly practised a technique to cut down negative inner dialogue and keep his attention present – he did this by stating to himself, 'I am the one who is walking down the beach / shooting the President / punching a nun' or whatever circumstance prevailed.

'Looka that,' muttered Thermidor, settling back again and gazing out the window. 'Every face flat as an owl from a lifetime collidin' with dead-end walls. All done out in their neighbour's image. That's a meekness of which I'm disposed to take a tolerant view, you understand. I tell ya, the breakup o' states couldn'ta come at a better time. You know sometimes a deal goes bad faster'n bananas but here entropy's an ally for guys who lead my kinda life.' He leaned forward again. 'Hey Sam, that's a fag car – instead of an airbag it deploys a giant Turkish delight. Gate the Eurocart so we got a clear shot, okay?'

Sam gunned the armoured limo. *I am the one who is ramming the Renault Megane*, he thought.

'That'll sow cress in their carpet, eh Sam?'

They were both thrown forward as the cars rear-ended.

'Eh, Sam? Hey, Bleaker, throw me a bone here.'

'I'm concentrating, boss.'

'I don't care about the state o' your bowels, Sam. This demonic wiseacres just picked up the groceries – when I'm through with him he'll be nuthin' short o' dead and buried in a hill o' beans.'

'Maybe you can't do that, boss.'

'I can too shoot him. What's not to shoot? Whattya mean?'

'Promise you won't get mad.'

'I promise nuthin'. I promise to kick your ass.'

'Just I heard Atom got shot one time in Fall Street and all hell broke loose.'

'Use your noodle, Sam. I tell ya no man governs his every breath. Not you, not even me. I'm gonna give ya the same advice somebody gave me many years ago. You can see somethin' in a man's eyes, okay – hatred, envy, delusions o' power – but it ain't no problem so long as there it stays. Him it messes with. Yeah, it's a crutch for salvation when you budget your vices like that. Me I got only one eye – and I keep it real clean.'

'Who gave yuh that kinda advice, boss – Coco the Clown?'

'Never you mind,' the boss snapped, thinking of his mother. 'Just bang the wheels out, hotrod.'

Sam 'Sam' Bleaker drew a pumped Mitsubishi, leaned it out the window and emptied both nostrils. The Eurocar sparked and swerved. *I am the one who is wasting ammo*, he told himself as he let rip, cranking between each blast.

'More uses for bones than burial,' said Dr DeCrow. Streetlight flashed across a face full of menace. 'Grind slowly the children – defeat is a fine holiday.'

'Whatever you say, mister,' said the cabby. As captain of an armoured Beerlight cab with a streetplough beak, he knew the delicate balance of power inherent in the enterprise. 'You want I should put on some music?'

'Authority takes everything. It nails the puddle of wine to the table.'

'Uh-huh.'

'There was once a bad divinity of shell and faith, which stacked heads in human view. The Bible never calms the urge to enforce purity. It falls far short.'

'I know what yuh mean.'

'But there's an out.'

'Yeah?'

'The *Hypostasis* tells us Samael is mistaken.'

'We all make mistakes.'

'Hell is a land of harmony in its own style. But without force the hierarchy is unsustainable. Take this gun.' DeCrow passed forward a small, oily Beretta 92F automatic pistol – the cab driver took it, glanced in the mirror and sighed deep with resignation, shaking his head.

'Fire upon the car in front, cabby. I'll retrieve that organ if you and me have to die trying.'

'You and me?'

'Pardon – you and *I*.'

The cabby rang up the gat meter, rolling his eyes and the window simultaneously. 'All right, mister – but you just wrecked deniability.' The first round romped home at 1,280 feet per second, licking the limo like a lover's ear.

'Scare up a couple or ten hotdogs, Benny,' mumbled Blince, biting into a burger.

'We're in a car, Chief. We're in pursuit.'

'Think I don't know that?' shouted Blince, thermals roaring off his face. 'I was escortin' speeders when you were soupin' your first tricycle. Christ, this one o' them burgers you bite down on if you're caught behind enemy lines?'

'We got gunfire, Chief,' said Benny, peering forward. 'Shells rocketin' round like Mexico City saucers.'

'Know what I like about a good old-fashioned patrol

stake, Benny? It's like entrapment but without the planning. Those rounds are flyin' in direct violation o' controlled airspace. See the limo? Twist the ignite in that mother you hear the choked-off laughter that greeted the first guy suggested puttin' fins on a vehicle. Money in the goddamn bank.'

'Givin' it some speed, Chief.'

'Bet your sweet life.' Blince lit a Hindenberg, drawing deep. He blew smog thoughtfully. 'I'll tell ya Benny, sponges are the lowest o' the low. Who else's skeleton would you put in your bath and refuse to acknowledge except to scrape off your own dead skin?' He took another draw. 'And by God, when we can't get one whatta we do? Rustle up a replica.'

'Eurocar's takin' a beatin', Chief. Rear's draggin' a bumper.'

Blince was frowning aside out the window. 'What's the purpose o' the human chin, Benny?'

'Guess a man's face gotta end somewhere, Chief.'

'Sounds to me like an admission o' defeat. That why we ain't evolvin' no more? Chin caps us like some kinda restraint?'

'You slay me, Chief.'

'Speakin o' which – I know you got ammo issues, Benny, but it's stone obvious you can't let your prejudices meddle with your duty here. Out your Ithaca, keep your heart behind your badge and don't ditch your guard.'

Blince spoke from experience. Back in cop training the Academy had sprung an actor firing Uzi blanks at the class to provide a subject for subsequent recall – in a lightning response, Blince had stood with a real Uzi and blown the actor away.

Driving one-handed, Benny drew his flaw and stuck his head into the night. He levelled at the studded cab and pulled. With no recoil and the report torn away by the wind, he had no idea whether the gun had discharged.

Something creased the roof over DeCrow's head as he watched the meter – the cabby had fired fifteen rounds and slapped in a fresh magazine, releasing another volley. Sam 'Sam' Bleaker was whipped across the arm, booming a fluke shot through the rear shield of the Eurocar and onward. Turow was shining in fear as something whanged against the panelling. He gibbered, weak and shrill. 'My nerves have rights – please let us slow down.'

Maddy glanced in the mirror and saw the starflare out a radiatored subgun. She went for a switch and deployed a cloaking system. Modern cloaking devices worked on a principle of denial allow. Unlike thermoptic camouflage, the denial cloak made a reading of whatever the onlooker could not afford to believe and sent out a microwave pulse mimicking that object. The onlooker refused to perceive it. But cars were a problem – not only were they too big for some people's psychological blind spot but they moved too fast to focus a sensor on the onlookers. Maddy had solved this by making her car into a subject of universal denial in actuality, not disguise. By hitting the switch, she flipped the car's propulsion to a cheap electric motor in the rear without any reduction in speed. For the pursuers something strange happened to Maddy's car. First the engine cut out – then the vehicle itself faded and vanished.

13

The Informer's Gift

'My apologies for having to do this uptown, Count. Hadda bring a barbecue up here t'escape the salivators – too many people swingin' visits to the pen. Just up the hall – Rex Camp's waitin' to suck up the ashes.'

DeCrow sat opposite in electrolock cuffs homed to a central computer. 'You mean the young man Fiasco?'

'Pretty soon,' rumbled Blince, lighting a cigar, 'they'll be firin' up that bad boy.'

A hoarse scream tore echoing through the uptown den.

'Was that it?' DeCrow asked.

'Nah, they're just shavin' his hair. Now, from the top – name.'

'I've always liked the name Tom Sawyer.'

'Well, Mr Sawyer, I "saw yer" doin' a hundred and ten in a stickle cab, whattya got to say about that?'

'Mr Blince, I was in the back of a taxi, at the back of a group of four vehicles. Why arrest me – why not the others?'

'In a gaggle o' four cars it's a cinch the guy at the rear knows who he's followin'. Why waste energy? Enough crime to supervise right now with the rod puppet's visit and the mob gettin' antsy. Lights on in the crime studio.'

'Blunder here and the gallows sprout, eh?'

'I like to think so, Mr Sawyer. What did that bastard

93

Wardial call it – "Beerlight City, jewel of asphalt". Real poetic, ain't it? Depravity's lotus land.' Blince paused, drawing on the cigar. The yelling cell was tamped down with unnatural silence during such pauses. 'But in the realm o' cold, hard, throbbin' fact, the sickness I've seen would shred your ears.'

A small smile further sharpened DeCrow's vulpine features. 'A man must be acquainted with the rugged incline of infinity before he can shred *my* ears.'

'Well howzabout this. A gal comes by, we don't notice her at first but then she gives it all up re Fiasco – says she thinks she's bein' followed by a mob boy. Five minutes after she quits the downtown den, the mob boy's head's nearly off, cut with a blade thin as theory. Terrible, tragic and so on. Shiv was so creepy he'd be furtive in a flood-light.'

'Tragic, as you say.' DeCrow nodded, his mouth slopping like a mudbubble. 'But not unusual. The female of the species, as they say. I'm an old man, Mr Blince. I remember when anger was merely a sign of haste. But consider humanity through the ages – my profession is archaeology, you understand. I study worlds bloodless as merry-go-rounds. Bricks sandwiching ancient air, cooked by the Aztec sun. I've seen battery insertion diagrams among Egyptian hieroglyphics. Crystal skulls barking yiddish punchlines. But such things are flavourless. I've resolved to live life and get the truth fresh out of the shell. Why, only last month I booted a cat off a fire escape. The pleasure it afforded me is hard to believe. Shortly thereafter I made a cool thousand, bowling with some of the larger jellyfish and sea anemones which are freely available in many fish markets. I laughed buckets, I can tell you. Of course, such amusement has an unremovable price tag. I was hounded from city to city, referred to as insane and charmless, and found myself here in Beerlight, a town about which I know practically nothing, and without the faintest idea where to strike next.'

'The corner exists for men like you, Sawyer. Go on.'

'Well. I began to hear of a dealer in bottled monsters by the name of Atom. You see, Mr Blince, I . . . Something I forgot to mention is the matter of my great tragedy. A son, long lost. The tales I heard of Atom led me to consider he might be the bairn I hadn't seen these twenty-five years. Yes, so I paid a cab driver by the hour to sit in wait for this Atom he knew by sight. And yet I don't know why I didn't think of it before – you, as Chief of Police, must know every denizen of this distorted metropolis. What news can you tell me of the boy?'

'So it's like that, eh? Well, Atom's got fan-forward rows of replacement teeth, like a shark. PI modality. Brownstone on Saints. Speaks eleven languages simultaneously. Searches the guards. Supplies trouble for them that want it. Purple barcode on his ass. Ask him his past and he'll smile enigmatic and tap the side of someone else's nose. Shot my mother's windchimes. Built a tugboat out of dead elves, because they said it couldn't be done. Only himself to blame. Those are the facts – but that's never the whole story, Mr Sawyer. We all know at a deep level how things should be. For instance it ain't natural to have a dog whose skull's bigger than your own. Something's wrong with this picture. Atom's father was a magician who'd make articles of food disappear by simply eating 'em. He never tumbled to why the crowd hated him – when they pelted him with fruit he caught it in his mouth and swallowed it. Then he varied his act, going into the audience – but instead of plucking eggs and pennies from onlookers' ears he tore off the ears and held them up with this look of . . . controlled exaltation them faggots always do. Next he started in on this ventriloquist act where he tried to convince the audience that the dummy could speak but just chose not to, because it didn't respect anyone present. Someone in the audience blew its head off with a rifle and Atom's dad was relieved that the charade was over at last. Then – and only then – did he tog up the four-year-old Atom in a dummy suit and a pink mask with a clacker jaw. Atom the toddler, hidden behind the hinge. And sat on his pa's knee, legs dangling motionless, that kid would chuck back the lines like a smart guy. Atom senior could drink a glass o' water, overlap the dialogue, you name it – got a real hilarious name for himself. But little Taffy became pretty sick o' bein' held by the neck every night, and during the act one evening he kicked off his dad's lap and ran amok in the club, jumping on to tables, biting holes in people's cheeks, setting fire to the curtains and squealing like a stuck pig. Afterwards, each witness described it a little differently. But all agreed on the presence of a demon. Atom senior was busted for possession, and died in the middle of a joke.'

'Which joke?'

'His life.'

'Ah-ha.' DeCrow smiled woodenly.

Blince gave a sour chuckle. 'You're pleasantly lifelike, Mr Sawyer – I could get to like you.' Blince relit his cigar. 'But I won't.'

'How exactly do you operate, Mr Blince?' DeCrow asked, throat crackling.

'Well now, tell me, d'you know the story o' the Walrus and the Carpenter?'

'Why no, I don't.'

'Good,' said Blince, and stared at him. The lights buzzed, guttered and blotted out.

Harry rode the lightning. The tangy fire which flared through his veins was like the embarrassment he felt when he saw a bad combo in the mirror. He was headed for the heart of the fourth of July.

Then he was with the guy Taffy Atom, on a platform over drooling sulphur. He was still strapped to the hotplate, which still resembled a low DIY table or self-surgery seat. Atom crouched to the same eye-level, his black coat pooling like tar. Fiasco noticed that the platform was chequered like a chess board. 'I don't play chess.'

'You do,' whispered Atom. 'I don't.'

'How's my hair, Atom? See, I'm a modern guy. My problems don't end with me, and I ain't about to smile.'

'Behind ugly data is a human way,' said Atom, his face slowly disappearing, 'mean and patched up, some doubts, hungry but very human.'

The sea of lava had become a planted field. Sunlight drew treasure glittering from the bulbs.

'America has the hallucinations it deserves,' Atom said, blue sky in place of his evaporated head.

'This is bad,' Fiasco muttered, feeling sick at the bioluminescent fields. Stuff like sap was linking up in his brain. Headlong the delivery of my failure, he thought, and black forgiveness washed over him.

'You had us concerned,' said his attorney, flaring out of a striplight blur.

Fiasco felt like a doll made of stone. He was in a pen cell. 'I baked or what?'

'Very nearly, Harry,' chuckled Specter. Rex Camp the Coroner stood behind him, benign but aloof in glasses which made his head look like a jukebox.

Fiasco found the bunk under him, sat up. 'Wha' happened?'

'A funny thing, actually. Geryon was on the lever, you were going with the flow, staring into the off, lights were dipping out – central brain at the den went down, in fact – when I got some real news. Someone confessed to your first crime.'

'So?'

'So no three strikes – you're down to two, so long as his story stands up. Guy called Flea Lonza.'

'I know Lonza.'

'How you see him?'

'Humble and no good.'

'Until now. Don't know why he's so keen to be swatched as a crook but I've offered to handle the publicity, which'll be almost as frenzied as yours truly's after the rescue. Shoulda seen it – I swanned into the steering room and whacked the lever like a last-ditch slab-arm, saving your scrawny ass. You took the equivalent of a mild course of ECT – you'll have periods of memory loss, flashbacks, bad concentration, and sometimes you'll just stand there.'

'I do feel kinda light-headed.'

Rex Camp had turned to leave, but stopped at the door and looked back at Fiasco. 'Later,' he croaked.

14

Europe After the Rain

The office of mayor suffered many opportunities to serve the people. These could be avoided by the use of a few key words passed to the elected on flagday. Meantime it was good to look busy – today the mayor was being chauffeur-driven to the McKenna Square Assembly Hall to present some sort of fuzzy-meaning item to the President. The mayor understood the rigours of electioneering – in the course of his own he had promised to establish a public holiday for the practice of gooey mid-lunge uncertainty, a ploy too cynical even for Beerlighters. His campaign slogan, 'Give dogs hell', did little to advance him. He finally had to trap the other three candidates in a cellar and smother them with his arse.

The matter of his aura had been concluded with a public statement that the office of mayor was not dependent upon public displays of spirit. Leon Wardial had responded with a seven-hour televised disintegration of the aura in an airport lounge.

Now the mayor hit the car TV and took a gander. Harry Fiasco, looking tan, was giving a statement in a sheetstorm of camera flash. 'How'd you feel?' someone asked.

'Modern, patched up, hallucinations bad, and I don't deliver. But I guess it's easy to be wise after the event. I . . . I promised myself I wouldn't cry. What I have to say is

99

this. One golfer a year is hit by lightning. This may be the only evidence we have of God's existence. When I was in the chair, I saw and felt stuff I don't fully recall. But I know we're all, every one of us here, ghosts in embryo. Predemons, I guess it is. And that's a real flowery way of saying, this here world's gonna end in fire and brimstone, ladies and gentlemen. Fire and brimstone for sure.'

A shot of Blince. 'This is the oldest tool in the box. Charmin' offender. Young enough to play victim. Fake epiphany in stir. Real touching. And once again the court authorities are slow as zombies changin' direction.'

Flea Lonza grinned uncertain at the camera as he was hustled through a hallway of yelling reporters.

'Why'd you steal that apple?'

'Yes, sir, I stole it – stole it good.'

'Why?'

Flea was shoved through a door. '– Hungry.'

The announcer spoke over shots of the President cutting a ribbon at a target range. 'The President underwent another blow to his banality with the revelation that every night he wraps gaffa tape around the head of a python and deepthroats it to the tune of "America" from *West Side Story*. We now go to Beerlight's McKenna Square Assembly Hall for the President's state address.'

The mayor leaned forward. 'Faster, driver – it's starting.'

The chauffeur turned around – under the formal cap was a woman of snow and smoke. 'Relax,' she said.

'What's the problem?'

She raised a gun at him. 'Metabolic.'

The blast woke him into a day that tasted of roses. Aimless stains of music in the air. Dwelling under leaves, hermits in the afternoon murmured, nights to reach in their praise. It was a barley-bronze country, revolting squirrels about oaks, garnet leaves across thirsty embankments, paladins and gaudy populaces beating through the countryside, poets tranced and petalled under clocks. Blue sugarpike dropped a hundred feet through the fall, spiralling at themselves over foam.

At dawn he selected eyeballs, a bagful of clinking trinkets, figurines of frozen blood. A large assemblage was milling its way under the diffused shadow of coppiced trees. The commanding welcome of colleagues, gentlemen slapping dead watches, laughter, quilltopped harlequins stroking strings. White fans under slow clouds. Stone banquets left in scatters. He paraded into the throne room and pierced the inquisition fuss, confronting the monarch. 'My liege,' he hollered, presenting the king with a tray of violet fungus tusks. 'Grind these and torch them in a bowl, see the flame colour and choose the morning shirt accordingly. But this, sire, is apparently what you do anyway.'

'It takes energy to curse someone. Waterlog this one's gullet merely.'

He walked a walk as a lion to the door, and after a swift backward glance, bolted. Holding air open to kick from the surroundings, he went across the gap of slates and lawns, gone behind him, flying over towers and tremendous monuments, tapering distances streaking into veins, places dashing out of sight. Trailing untidiness overwashed the geology, riddling green to the coast. Tropical boats of crowds, blue and red garments, hot drops of deep summer, delusions seeping from nectar as amazon poison. He led voiceless science into the mountains, pointed to land under faded clouds, pushed . . .

Then he swallowed the gods and slept, dreaming he was the mayor of a nightmare city, lying dazed in an oily alleyway.

The President took the stage with a floodlight smile and

foxhole eyes. His frosted hair was an icepack for an angry boil of a head. A thunder of backhands greeted his arrival.

Campaign bluster slowly narrowed to a finer focus. 'There are pips in the fruit of liberty,' he stated. 'They are called elections. Banners make the man. I have spearheaded the important transition from a government unconcerned with the people's endorsement to one which takes their endorsement for granted. I'm determined to complete this transition, however unpopular. I don't intend to establish a beachhead and then squander it on damn pelicans.'

After applause the mayor was announced and when Atom walked on in an allow cloak, everyone denied their eyes – they'd been told this was the mayor so it must be at any cost. He needn't have bothered – the turnover in mayors was so fast nobody could keep pace with their names or appearance. 'Mr President,' Atom said expansively, 'that was a finely crafted speech. I'm sure every bastard here will join me in thanking you. And before you go on back to hell I'd like to present you with a modest token of our complicity. Myself and the powers that be have thought long, hard and veined about what might be appropriate. Something symbolic, perhaps? Some kinda dumb trophy? We had a good laugh about that. But it was decided to give you something you really need. So here's a brain, in a kind of icebox. Take pleasure in it.'

Atom handed over the cryo box and the President, beaming, opened it up. Amid applause he and Atom shook hands for the blaze of camera strobe, the box tilted like a presentation plaque. 'Mr President,' said Atom through the clench of his grin, 'the day that Memorial statue of Abe Lincoln looks aside with a great wrench and steps down like a Harryhausen giant, your balls are pancakes.'

ATOM'S JOURNAL

Owl with a face like an intake fan. A filigree of golden ductworks, sweating with rootwater. A giant rabbit in the wheelhouse of a missing container ship, staring ahead, woffling its nose, ignoring the state-of-the-art direction-finding equipment. A mirrorcool sky. Scattering rain. A planted field, just beginning to crack.

15

One in the Eye for Justice

Harpoon Specter closed a case of non-shedding lizard skin and stood to secrete his summation. Flea Lonza had a helpless look in his eyes. This was meant to be his show but he felt he'd been dismissed like yesterday's air.

'We gather here,' said Specter, striding slow, 'to tell salty tales around the campfire of our spite. To open up a treasure chest of memories while weeping bitter tears of valediction. To make some sense of this force ten error we call our lives.'

The judge, a figure of squashed grey putty, crumpled. 'God almighty, Specter,' he said, gripping his own face in an effort to recover, 'break it right down and tell us – what's your argument?'

'Promise not to laugh?'

'Modesty's kinda useless if everyone agrees with you, Specter – don't test it.'

'We're all learning, your honour. There may even be a lesson for us in the roaring pep-rally of circumstantial evidence my learned adversary chooses to term his case. It's to my client's everlasting credit that he hasn't slaughtered the lot of us right here for being this dumb and slow. Biting us if he has to. A competent attorney could establish the shocking facts in two of your Earth minutes, ladies and gentlemen of the jury. And I've been tempted to expedite matters by flirting shamelessly with the lot of you – especially you, madam. Yes, you with the big hair. Don't speak, it's not permitted. Yes, ladies and gentlemen, I'm tempted to inject your tax dollars into the belly of the first juror I see to save my client. But let us not take the short route home. Let us not put this to rest, only to awaken to a breakfast of errata. We must scrape the flies from the headlamps of truth, then switch the fuckers to high beam. Oh, don't get me started on that one.' Specter paused before the jury, seeming to ponder. He closed the curtains on his heart, fastening a button. 'I'm reminded of the Bible story in which the shepherds couldn't stop laughing. And the angel Abrasaks asked them, "Why are you laughing?" And the shepherd who could pull himself briefly together replied, "As below, so above." History is replete with working stiffs like you and me being lashed for our humanity by goons with eyes lost in science. Is sin as irreversible as a botched sculpture? Can we steal the remedy? Take a look at Flea Lonza over there, ladies and gentlemen of the jury. Look at that front-loading face, incapable of conscious deception. His expression, like that of a man who has just bitten into wax fruit. His ears like air brakes. We've all laughed at Flea's ears at least once. Some of us have joined several such hacking out-bursts together to form a volley or "peel" of hilarity. But few would deny they're a godsend to an informant. And make no mistake, that's what he is. A big-eared psycho like his father before him.'

'Mr Specter,' said the judge, and paused to gather and present his thoughts. 'You realise, Mr Specter, you're the defence attorney? You're meant to be arguing in the way of innocence regarding your client? What's so exciting about the man's ears?'

'Well that's the real question, isn't it, your honour?

Context is everything. Take a dead, dry molecule from an orange, balance it on your finger – utterly useless to one and all. But put it in a box of granola, and it's gold dust. People'll seek it out. And so must you, ladies and gentlemen of the jury. You have heard my client's apparently sincere opinion that he boosted fruit. The arresting officer was Lung Mussolini, whom we must assume knows what he's doing. You have heard expert testimony that no man could have approached the fruit stall on Posford Street without being visible. We've seen math, sightlines, theory. And a parade of likely perverts with the strutting arrogance to claim they can recall the fashionable events of a day two years ago. Who do they point to? Super Ears over there. Should these contradictions crowd goodness into a cell? If so, let man return to the pockets of the volcano.'

Specter digressed into Nash-Wardial Theft Theory, which calculated the amount stolen as diametric to self-worth in a moral man and diametric to morals in a man of self-worth, concluding that in stealing a single apple Flea had proven himself a man of either high morals or rockbottom self-esteem. Either way, he deserved the jury's sympathy. And Specter was swaggering now. 'Still a young man and you'd have him cross himself while holding a knife. Well, let me tell you the story of another young man. Drove a diesel van and went by the name of Atom. Supported his little son Taff by hauling facts across Our Fair State. That's right, a double-edge like Flea here, set on the crooked path by a shove off the school insignia. Fated to provide Rex Camp with a thousand-piece puzzle. Remember the McDougal cop cell assassination? Atom Senior knew who did it but unlike the rest of us, he went to the *Daily Denial* in the early hours, only to find his appointed rendezvous with a hack a mere rendezvous with death. The lone soul in the office was a government mechanic who immediately pulled a sender and let rip. The gore impact activated the fax machine, transmitting the splash pattern to a programmed number, fixing time, place, trajectory and interpretive psychological demeanour via the blot form. Conspiracy theorists later claimed it showed healthy affection and appropriate respect for the assassin's mother. The assassin panicked, shifted the angle of the fax and bolted. He was about to turn himself in when he heard the fax had gone directly to the White House, so that was the end of that. Or could have been if he hadn't bragged of his good fortune at a party. A concerned citizen overheard him, went to the cops, and was assassinated. Little orphan Atom passed this story on to Flea with its lesson intact. Flea never passed to a hack, he never passed to the brotherhood, knowing that the edge who blabs is inevitably blunted.' Specter leaned forward on the jurors' box. 'Here are the teeth that forgot to bite – here are the written rights of man.' He fixed the jurors with a significant stare. 'Don't go down that road, ladies and gentlemen. It'll be cigarettes for supper and a stroll to the mercy seat. And I don't buy that. The only way my client could have approached that applecart is vertically down the face of the wall using some part of his anatomy as suction cups. Needless to say, nobody thought to dust that wall for prints. It's absurd, why should they? Unfortunately for the barnacle-encrusted prosecution, the lack of such evidence leaves the case as we see it today – a construction as lurid and irrational as a stalker's shrine.'

'Your honour,' said the prosecution, bolting up. 'I request a continuance.'

The judge looked like a guy in a headache commercial. 'The trial is over, counsellor.'

Specter raised his hand. 'I wasn't finished, your honour.'

16

A Dream

'Taff,' said Jed Helms, sculling his deep body in the office tank. 'I think I had a dream.'

He blinked his lantern-eyed head, light blotches rippling over jet barbs and silver pain cells.

'The office, the trap, the whole city was flooded with water. I could go anywhere – I was free.'

Atom was leaned back in his chair, hands behind his head, watching the ceiling fan. 'Maddy says maybe you're overcompensating for your short kill range.'

'Maybe. I know Maddy's still workin' on them water-proof cigars, a bigger tank and all. But since this caper with the headberries, the Fort and that dip in the hot tub with Cherry and Linda, I got me a broader swatch.'

'You ate dip? Well, that's all over now. I got rid of the crap axis, everyone owns their own problems. We got downtime. I ever tell you about my dad?'

'A million times.'

The desk light flashed, and a moment later a guy swanned in who seemed to have died but continued to move out of sheer malice. Sleek and shiny as a beetle (Atom wondered if he'd rot down as fast), he goggled in a perfunctory way at the principal objects in the room and commenced to rasp a tubercular protest over the prow of a Beretta 92F. 'Do you know what you've done?'

'Tell me – I've forgotten.'

'You had in your grasp one of the keys to the survival of our intelligence, and you – you give it to the *President*?'

'It's like that sometimes.'

'Like what exactly? Anyone near gets flipped into negative, is that it? The sheer sit-up-and-watch stupidity of your actions, your unbridled arrogance, these mental wedgies you use for communication, this empty place with one office, that lurid lobby? You're naked! Are you mad?'

'Isn't it terribly expensive?' Atom tapped a shock from a packet and lit it up. 'I oughta install a revolving door in here, number of people come in to lay down their stuff from back of a snub.'

'What I have to say is too important to relate with my gun sheathed.'

'So shoot, if you can.'

'To be dared is to be shown the poverty of the darer's vision.'

Atom saw the gun shivering. This desiccated ghoul had been knocked sideways but his eyes were flat with malevolence. It was like being watched by something you just put in the garbage.

'While we perch here fronting off, that cryo hamper's heading outta town. Because I didn't like any part of it,' Atom added before DeCrow could ask, and stabbed out his shock on the desk. 'Get you and the gent, swappin' noggins like baseball cards – is that any way for grown men to behave?'

'You bloody fool,' hissed DeCrow. 'The brain in the freezerbox isn't Kafka's. I performed surgery before that hayseed Fiasco thought to steal it. Kafka's brain is in the Candyman's head.'

'What?'

'Yes,' DeCrow gloated. 'Who's naked now? Think of it, Atom – after such extended suspension it was vital to get blood through that brain. And who would think to look for it there? This was the first phase of the operation. The second was to fuse part of the Candyman's mind back into the cranium, and finally to fit the body with a chitinous carapace. Turow knew nothing of this.'

'And before you could do it, Fiasco boosted the Candyman's skull tackle, thinking he was stealing the bonce he'd taken earlier from the Brain Facility. So how did the gent lumber and chortle with his brain in a station stash box?'

'The freezercase is wired with a wet cerebral interface, its signal microwaved to a receptor in the Candyman's spine. The system was temporary, Atom, and the signal finite. When the Candyman's brain leaves Our Fair State, the brain now residing dormant in his skull will take over. *Now* do you see what you've done, you complacent maniac?'

'A choice between some buggy-thinkin' patrician decked out like a bunker tank or a thin man in a slob's body, it's jake with me. The gent cut loose, didn't he? Likely suspected you were planning to take his body and K's qoph as soon as you were sure K was in the pink. And when the gent left the hotel you'd been usin', the handle on him was the brain in that cryo box. You really dropped the ball on this one, didn't you? You've been lurchin' round town followin' every lead as inconspicuous as a pig in a minefield – all for your precious chiggers.'

'Bugs shall prevail amid blowing embers, Mr Atom. As idiots prevail in this cauldron of malice and—'

'You're right at home, Doc – except for the unexpected. You can't handle that. You're the conformist from the black lagoon. Bet you didn't imagine the crime string knotting up this way when you coded it. You bore the hell outta me.'

'This bullet will.'

The door banged open behind DeCrow and the Candyman lolled in, slurring. 'I should have known it, sir,' he said, trying to focus on Atom. 'You've drawn the true venom here. Did you know that he practises on himself. Great globules in the alleys, sir, I could give you chapter and verse on his depravity . . .'

No longer cheerful and impervious, he drifted off momentarily, glancing about as if unsure of it all.

'You on line, Candyman?' asked Atom.

'. . . in this rolling disaster you call the world. A refusal defines you amid moving cruelty. Full marks, sir . . .' He toppled against the wall and slid heavily to the floor, his voice fluttering feebly. '. . . a premature breaking-off of methodical procedure . . . and under the scene, ants swarm like electrons . . . no more torture . . . why continue . . .' He looked up real pathetic, his veering accent a weakened whine. Maybe time and neglect had done its work on his mind, but K's first clear statement was 'I never cribbed from Gogol.' His spirit was spiked with poison. 'Any more than Schulz cribbed from me. And I never heard of Zamyatin!'

'See that?' barked DeCrow, pointing with the gun.

'Why you so bent outta shape – you got what you want, ain't you? Right there. Hey, K, Brod really did a number on your will, didn't he? You'll be glad to hear he's dead.'

'This really is America,' K muttered, standing unsteadily.

'How's it feel?'

'Like it was built last week.'

'Yeah. You been aware of stuff while the gent was at the wheel?'

'Mostly. The bone of another man's forehead blocks my way. And I'm fat – I can't disappear.'

'Guess it musta been real frustratin',' said Jed from the tank, 'bein' able to look out on the world but not act in or affect it.'

Kafka gave him a look of bafflement and dawning contempt.

'K's a rowing machine, Jed,' said Atom.

'He sounds like a girl,' Jed observed.

'What in hell is *this*?' gasped DeCrow, peering into the tank. 'Did you build this yourself? Is it sentient? A hybrid?'

'See why I wanted to conclude this, Jed?'

'You're right, it stinks.'

'Wanna go fishing?'

They were still laughing about that when the phone rang. 'Excuse me, fellas,' said Atom and flipped the tumbler. 'Yeah, Maddy.'

'Thermidor thinks he's kidnapped me,' she told him.

'Where are you?'

'Candyman's room at the Bird.'

'How'd he find the lab?'

'He didn't – I was visiting Flea at the pen, they got me in the lot.'

'Deployed anything?'

'Didn't want to bloody my pants, Taff. Come on over.'

'Knew if we hung around Atom's place we'd swatch Houdini's husk. Sawyer's skeleton clicks like a boiler dial.' Long estranged from his own skeleton, Blince was damning in his assessment of others'. The stakeout had borne fruit.

'D'you make Atom for Sawyer's breaker or like that? System went down, Chief – the cuffs popped.'

'Maybe, maybe not. Need arms like twigs to slip 'em but

Sawyer's a freak. Those cuffs were closed when the lights came up, Benny. So was the goddamn door, and Sawyer took a powder. Then he winds up here brownbaggin' some kinda snub – same one the cabby described maybe. Where'd it go between times? He swallow it? Real convenient.'

Only their heads extended above the patrol car's doughnut level. They were like drowning giants pelted with lifebelts.

'Ever notice you never see Jesus and Oliver Hardy in the same room? I the first to suspect somethin' here?'

'Usually are, Chief. Who was the arbuckle went in after?'

'Seen it all before – Atom's a catalyst. Doesn't change. Maybe I'll respect that.'

'Respect it for why?'

'For why's a kamikaze pilot wear a goddamn helmet? I don't make predictions, Benny, and I never will.'

'So what's the real story with Atom?'

'Got into some noble scrape and went away burdened with gifts he had to wield with honour, what I heard.'

'Someone's comin' out, Chief.'

Three figures emerged from Atom's brownstone. A cloaked cadaver cradling its gored face, followed by a naked Atom and the fat gent carrying a fishtank between them. In the tank's gloom rocked a giant mouth with a tail. Atom's voice carried to the cop car. 'Self-surgery eh, Professor? Real fashionable. Remember, Jed, chew at least ten times. Right, K?'

'Well now, bless my soul,' Blince rumbled. 'Looka that, Benny. Don't let anyone tell you idealism's dead.'

17

The Girl Who Was Death

'You want order in this world,' muttered Maddy, surveying the roomful of milling detainees, 'there's the refrigerator.'

'Think Atom'll come for you?' asked Kitty on the couch next to her. She was retouching her lipstick with a spraycan.

Madison concealed her surprise – she hadn't known Kitty was here. 'There's no evil in Atom for long,' she said. 'What is it with you and Fiasco?'

'Kinda love-hate thing – he loves me and I hate him. Honey's harder'n Harry's heart.'

'Eh?'

'I said softer'n a boiled smurf. He's a dreamer but don't know it. When you're dreaming you don't know you're dreaming, right? He's a kinda hayseed?'

'How does he see you?'

'As somethin' I ain't.'

'That's not what I meant, honey.'

'Uh? Oh, yuh mean how people pretend I ain't there sometimes? Yeah, I guess he ain't so superior that way.'

'So where'd you choose your face?'

'This here newspaper clippin',' said Kitty, taking a frail bit of parchment from her handbag. 'I don't recall the story but ain't she classic glam?'

'Mother!' shouted Thermidor, spotting the photo. 'When

she was young – it's the picture they printed with the obits at the end of her life!' And he exploded into sobs.

At last, about ten o'clock at night, Atom came to the door of the hotel room and was let in carrying the fish-tank with the K man, Dr DeCrow entering ahead of them.

'So the gang's all here,' Thermidor declared, pouring a Jacad Splash at the drinks counter. 'Don't be a stranger, Atom.'

'Can't help that. I'm glad you're making new friends, Thermidor.' Atom saw Turow sitting morose in a corner. 'Goin' back over, eh?'

Turow squirmed. 'No, it was getting quite late, and . . .' Then he saw DeCrow. 'What is *he* doing here? Do not trust him, Mr Candyman, don't listen to anyone.'

DeCrow sneered. 'This isn't the Candyman, you dolt. Your master left you to the birds when I popped the hood and pulled his brain – two hours after Fiasco returned from the Facility. The brain in this candy-coloured clown is Kafka's.'

'He lied,' Turow seethed. 'He lied to me! Even as he opened that accursed icebox!'

'Guys, guys!' Thermidor laughed. 'Stow it – I'm gettin' chafed in the crossfire here! I been growin' tusks gettin' us all together in one place so don't be gettin' your asses in an uproar, eh? You all know me. This is the wrecking crew for tonight – Cortez the Killer.'

'Yo,' said Cortez.

'Sam "Sam" Bleaker.'

I am the one who is being introduced by the boss, thought Sam.

'And Silencer.'

Silencer moved his lips without a sound.

'If you look real hard you may detect Miss Invisible

World, Kitty Stickler. Sadly a doll is warm by association only.'

'If I weren't a lady I'd kick your teeth in.'

'Yeah, but you'd look pretty dumb in that dress. Then shivering in the corner we got Mr Turow, a gripewater. Squirtgun scared but functional.'

Turow looked wretched.

'Joanna, a strongarm grown in a polythene tunnel.'

'Naughty naughty,' Joanna chuckled.

'The guy without no clothes is Taffy Atom, a joker.'

'Boy, you know right where to pour the vinegar.'

'The mutant fish is a bit player.'

'Any port in a storm,' bubbled Jed.

'The wildcat's Madison Drowner, and she's an interesting case. All I know for sure is she ain't askin' anyone's approval. Take my advice you'll seek mine.'

'You can store your advice in a cool, dry place.'

'The lurching corpse over there, old sparrow hands, I ain't sure what that is. Seen somethin' like it in old movies with test tubes and electrical storms. And its fat friend's got the look of a guy who owes somebody. That turbulence behind the eyes.'

Fat Kafka was sat on a wooden chair by the fishtank. He looked up startled, defensive. 'To my best knowledge, I owe nothing. All right, so I took bribes from the legal profession to go easy on them in *The Trial*, and a deal's a deal, isn't it? I held up my half. Did I hurt anybody? Why are you staring at me? Do I seem such a suspicious character? Do you think I wished to fetch up in this place? It is not what I imagined! Where are the singing voices? The unity? This is the black burden of truth! Time is longer than hope! Time is longer than hope!' He gripped his head. 'The cool knife through the paper-thin integument of the working brain!' And he twisted to the floor, convulsing.

'I *like* this guy!' gasped Turow.

'Near time to make our move, Benny – let whatever's developin' up there stew into full flavour. Remember the cliché murders, Benny? Put 'em in reality, see how they stood up? Reminds you folk in this town care more about the quality o' crime than the quantity. Only time I found a serial interestin'.'

'About a year ago, right, Chief?' said Benny, at the wheel. 'Guy locked in a basement, only way to haul himself up to the window was with a couple o' bootstraps.'

'Sure. Flies and stench alerted the authorities. Found rattle-eyed and flesh all gone to custard.'

'Then there was the guy staked down in that field during a storm, lightning conductor in his back, struck over and over.'

'And the guy who lost his life on the swings, near a roundabout. But the one that pecks at my pulsin' brain is the smoke without fire setup. Guy in a locked house, dry ice machine on, sprinklers on, house fillin' with water. If the smoke was caused by fire the sprinklers would put it out and shut off, right? But the smoke detectors wouldn't even start out on ice smoke, Benny.'

'Right again, Chief – them sprinklers were jammed on manually.'

'Killer shoulda used an off-beam friction motor.'

'Yep, he faked it.'

'But you know, Benny, it occurs to me the cliché was disproved when we volted that guy in the chair.'

'Why? Cos o' that wisp o' smoke off his head or the fact he was the wrong guy?'

'Both, Benny, that's the beauty o' the thing. Okay, I reckon it's time.'

'Don't know which room they're in, Chief.'

'Let's simplify matters – call for backup, Benny.' Blince opened the car door – a clogging avalanche of doughnuts tumbled into the street. He gazed up at the Bird Street Hotel through the smoke of his cigar. It was a good night for containment. Anticipation sent ripples across his star-spangled heart. He raised the bullhorn. 'Listen up in the Bird Hotel. You're all under false arrest. File yourselves out in an orderly fashion.'

There were eighty rooms in the Bird Street Hotel. Within each a tableau froze in surprise – grocers laminating the ears of a shuffling baby elephant, a clown tearing a crucifix from the neck of a doubting priest, a sales demonstration of a cop-issue garrotting bar, a rifle-point pie-eating contest, a faceless man manufacturing codeine ice cream in a thundering drum, a dour meeting of a gun quitters' support group, a porcelain dog screaming muted and inarticulate, lovers acting out an alien abduction, the execution of a dirtbiker by firing squad, grans sat laughing before a wind turbine, a rabbi punching through a man's hat, a kelp fisherman branding a crosshair bullseye in the centre of his forehead, a rickety old man snogging a lion made of sponge, sniggering spaniels concocting ever more lurid parasol drinks, a historian listening to Zapata's death screams on a wax drum, a cleaner unknowingly sucking her guardian angel into the dustbag, galoshered senators filling their pants with high-pressure wall cavity foam – all halted and stared aside at Blince's blared announcement. Then as one they burst from the hotel, guns blazing. First through the door were the gun quitters' support group. The cop car was tearing to tin streamers. Blince and Benny crouched behind it counting their ammo like small change. 'How many gunners, Benny?'

'Sixty-four. And an old lady throwing stones.'

'Bless her. Right-handed or left?'

'Both, Chief.'

'That's community spirit.' The roofsparker was blasted away by a volley which Blince didn't dignify with a return shot. 'Gets me thinkin' how people get confused. Maybe the word "left" belongs with the right hand.'

'Howdya mean, Chief?' yelled Benny over the commotion.

'Everyone knows left and right are wrong. Right should actually be called left, and what we call left is another word altogether. Howdya like *them* apples?'

'Ready, Chief?'

'Ready.' Blince cycled his snub. 'I'll take the left, you take the right.'

They stood from behind the wreck and fired to the right, killing the old woman. A window went up on the third floor and Eddie Thermidor stuck his head out. 'Keep the noise down – some of us are tryin' to live our lives up here!'

'Eddie Thermidor!' called Blince. 'Sawyer up there?'

'I guess you did.'

'Chief Blince,' said Atom, appearing naked at the window. 'They're setting jello in the shape of a sailor – help me.'

'The rest o' you can go your sweet way,' hailed Blince at the shooters. The firing petered out and the crowd, muttering, began straggling back into the hotel. 'I want all you up in that room – front and centre.'

18

Out of Space

Cop cars were tearing up and howling like loons. 'Hear that?' said Atom. 'Blince is a cop flushed down the pan and grown huge in the sewers. His insanity's a matter of public record. We got only minutes to get set for the yelling cells.'

'What are you drivin' at, shamus?' snapped Thermidor. 'What are you drivin' at? What gives you the credentials to take the wheel?'

'I told you, we're sitting on dynamite. The one time Blince got near a fact his hair caught fire. Now these fashionable events can be explained in a way which could work in our favour and I believe I can perform the deep stitching required. We can bolster the credence later. You see, it's the details that lodge in the discriminating mind. It's true, isn't it? The easiest way to start out is to make use of a wrong. And don't go for something lame. Look at your gatman Cortez, flaw drawn, eyes like a surlyguy bust, stubble like a sticklebrick. In four to six years he'll head the mob, in seven he'll be crazier than a shithouse rat and the leftovers'll go to Betty. We can use that. Young blood on the ascendant, lotta stiffs, we need a fall guy.'

'I don't like that,' said Cortez tightly.

'Neither do I,' muttered Thermidor slowly, squinting at Cortez. 'Atom, how d'you survive more than a minute crackin' this wise?'

'I don't know,' Atom conceded. 'It worries me, actually.'

'You *oughta* worry.'

'Okay, okay. So Cortez doesn't step off. How 'bout Joanna here?'

'The lummox? This cornfed waterhead?'

'Why not? Sure he's in a biological no-man's-land but that makes him the perfect blank for the cops' impression. Look at him. He's the one for that. Dumb and visible, shaves with a sandblaster – can't say fairer than that, can we? We'll tell them over and over that he masterminded the whole thing. Then we let the tide come in on him.'

'Yuh really think this all-terrain moron's our ticket outta here?' asked Thermidor. 'What's the motive?'

'Well, let's see.'

'I like bunny rabbits,' offered Joanna.

'There you go – Joanna wanted to quit the loop to start a rabbit home in the country, and for that he needed money. He attached a limpet mine to his arse and entered the stronghold demanding a substantial sum in return for your survival. You mocked him, called him a clown, threw a sprout at him, even. Joanna pulled the ripcord but the mine flubbed and the entire mob erupted into mocking laughter. Joanna said – remember this, Joanna – "You'll pay for this" and fled weeping into the night.'

' "You'll pay for this",' frowned Joanna. 'For the rabbits?'

'Stow it, cracker,' snapped Thermidor.

'Let him alone,' muttered Kafka, then repeated it at a yell.

'As he passed the Brain Facility the mine went off,' Atom continued, 'knocking the building flat but leaving Pro-Magnon Hitman here standing. And who ran by at that moment but Harry Fiasco. Knowing he was a mob boy, Joanna brought him into a scheme to draw the cops down on Thermidor, the man who'd mocked him.'

'Oh, it's ridiculous,' muttered Mr Turow vaguely. 'Why ever would Fiasco do that?'

'Because Joanna saw him wearin' spandex. Spandex which you forced upon him, Turow, having trapped him in a steel corral on the outskirts of the city. With a dozen other unfortunates. Only he escaped, and you couldn't take that. You chased him in a serrated armoured car like a giant grater. And you kept on pursuing him as Joanna's plot proceeded. The assigning of value to a random object, something he found on the ground, a brain. Stir a fuss around it – get Thermidor to think it's the true and only spice. Get Harry sent up with his story, pointing to the mob. And meanwhile folk are goin' oblong all over town. That was you too, eh, Joanna? And you let every telltale ingredient simmer, till any killing initiated naturally garnered the hell experienced policemen invariably store snug amid their sadness for just such a time.'

'So what was I doin' through all this?' asked Thermidor.

'Carving tiny little firearms for doll's houses. With your one eye you're a dab hand at that kinda close work. You were seeking a patent for the notion when Fiasco was arrested, breaking your flow. Sam "Sam" Bleaker can attest to the night you dressed up as Santa Claus and wept till your beard dropped away like heated snow, berating aloud the tender complexity of the human heart.'

Sitting on the edge of an armchair, Sam "Sam" Bleaker baby-dandled a gun on his knee. He frowned. 'Then what did I do?'

'You gave him a marshmallow. Then you went to Silencer over here and said, "That'll keep him busy for a while", and you both went sniggering for a naked mid-night swim. That was the real start of your love for each other. The next day you were married in secret. As the priest mumbled words misleading and sacred, you saw yourselves as dryads of combat, heroes abandoned by moral hurry. Your death-hemmed, bloodshot eyes closed upon each other that evening in the beauty of dumb luck and exhaustion. You're closer than heaven and hell, and you'd go to the mat for each other.'

Sam "Sam" Bleaker looked at Silencer, who moved his mouth silently. Sam turned to Atom. 'He says he can't swim.'

'Let that slide.'

'What I do after eatin' the mallow?' asked Thermidor.

'You fell into a deep sleep,' Atom explained. 'And you dreamt you were being crowned king in some ancient ceremony. Even as the crown descended, a rainbow butterfly flittered across the scene and was trapped between the crown and your undead hair. To remove it would disturb the routine and so the beauty was ignored amid the grey blare to its expiry. Deeply affected, you woke with a plan to have yourself declared an official currency and read your worth every day in the rags. You entered an elevator and told a man reading such a rag that over and above everything, charm was out. "Indeed," said this guy urbanely, turning a page. "I run a dog pound." Your stomach turned over as the elevator slowed to a stop, the lights dimming briefly. "Hello," says the man, "must be pumping out a dungeon." The man's taking a watermask and breathing apparatus from his briefcase and strapping it on, adjusting the mouthpiece and bracing himself. "What's going on?" you shout. The man looks round at you and, surprised, says something incomprehensible, pointing at his aqualung. He's shaking you by the shoulders when water starts trickling from the doorcrack and dripping from the ceiling. The man points at the door in explanation as the trickle becomes a spray which fans and widens. The man picks up his briefcase and stands in the deepening water. You stand in the corner, sobbing. The newspaper frills and drifts in the tide. The lights go out and the man says something through his mouthpiece. The water's up to your knees and you wade to another corner, feeling the wall in pitch blackness. You reach up and the ceiling moves easily at your touch – you hear a hatch rattle and bang like the lid of a biscuit tin. Punching it open, you jump and clasp on to the edges, hoisting yourself up and gasping with your exertions. The man begins protesting through his mouthpiece and pulling at your legs. Kicking downward and struggling through, you stand and look about you. A dazzling light's shining in your eyes, and you hear gasps of laughter from somewhere in front of you. You stumble forward and shield your eyes, finding with dismay that you're standing on a theatre stage before a large audience. Sensing your embarrassment they grow silent and apprehensive – some snigger cruelly. You shuffle forward, your pants sopping wet. "Where's the hotel?" you demand. To your surprise, the audience roars with laughter, and some of them even applaud. You squint down at the prompter's box – tears of hilarity stream down the prompter's face. You look out once again at the auditorium. "I have lost my way," you state. Shrieks of mirth echo about the theatre – you peer about for the exit as the laughter subsides, and bang on the backdrop with your fists. "Let me out of here," you shout, furious. The audience roar, and when you go over and kick the prompter in the mug, you get 'em rolling in the aisles. Some are bent into impossible contortions across the backs of chairs, shuddering with hysteria. "What kinda place is this?" you demand. You leap from the stage and grab someone in the audience by the scruff of the shirt, but lower your fist on seeing the man's so helpless with laughter he couldn't answer you if he wanted to. You dash up the centre aisle, and a few people try to touch you as you pass – even the doorman chuckles tearfully, expressing his gratitude between gasps. Everyone seems to have nothing but admiration for you. Outside the theatre house there's posters of you everywhere, grinning and wearing a top hat. It's night, raining, and you hail a cab. When you're off and you mention where you wanna go, the driver tells you the hotel was destroyed twenty years ago by Chinamen. "Pardon me?" you ask, leaning forward. The driver tilts around – he's got the rotten head of a goat. White foam's about its teeth and its eyes are turned upward in its head. Tyres begin squealing and the driver wobbles lifelessly as the car mounts the sidewalk and plunges into a storefront. A burglar alarm's ringing and distant dogs bark as you stumble out of the wreckage and through a shower of water geysering from a hydrant. Detail, Thermidor, you see what I'm saying?'

'Wait a minute this is my *life* we're talkin' about here,' Thermidor protested. 'I'm awake and what happens?'

Atom ignored him. 'In all fairness to Joanna he bolstered his hand with Kitty over there, telling her if she gave false data on Harry he'd tell her a foolproof way ahead in life, a way to use the gifts she's got instead of the gifts she thinks she's got. Deal's a deal, as the K-man says.'

'You sayin' I got the cops on to Harry?'

'I'm giving you an out.'

Kitty snorted. 'Listen, buster, I never told a thing, not one thing.'

'Sure, angel. But what's more he said if you don't shoot your mouth off he'd tear you down like a curtain and leave you facedown in regret. You felt . . . how would you feel?'

'So I'd feel . . . I guess I . . . felt trapped?'

'Trapped, sure. Like candy in a store window. Of course you spouted, and got your reward.'

'Well what kinda big wisdom did this guy give me?'

Kitty challenged him, interested now. Atom came over and leant to her ear, whispered, and moved away again. Kitty's laughter was cold and happy as a dawn.

'So what about the fat guy?' demanded Thermidor.

Kafka, jealously admiring Kitty's ability to evade the eye, was startled when the mob boss pointed at him.

'He's nothing,' Atom stated, 'irrelevant – you could shoot a dozen like him in any corner drugstore. His only distinction is his former champion status in the noble art of British gut-barging, in which his ring name was "Bigbelly Head Charge" or "The Fender". He came to prominence at the turn, and was known for the pre-match taunting of his opponent with the bellowed phrase "I consider that I am significantly better than you at gut-barging". His victory swan-dives into the audience were legendary in the annals of personal injury litigation. He was network gold until he was kidnapped and placed on an enforced diet, then released slender and fit minutes before a fight. The appearance of this quailing reed in the ring was the beginning of the end in the media's eyes and now, despite pigging out for years, he's reduced to opening stores in his old glitter belts. In the wrong place at the wrong time, he found himself being embroiled in dismal conversation with Turow, who was by now hanging on to a frayed rope over a yawning chasm of personal failure. Attempting to escape he dressed up as a woman but just looked like a lamp on steroids. His photograph was taken and used on the cover of a specialist magazine, and for shame he cannot leave this small room. Thermidor forced entry with the crowbar of kindness, searing the sufferer with his charity. Sam "Sam" Bleaker and Silencer danced attendance while Cortez waited in the wings to strike, and Joanna and all his coerced crew descended like a hard rain on the innocent Eddie. Jed's here as food, Maddy's here as witness to our folly, and the ghost of George Washington lives in the thermostat. Something for everybody, eh, K-man?'

'So the galoot steps off. What do we do with Turow?' asked Thermidor.

'Drown him in rosewater.'

'Why you—' Turow tussled with himself, petulant and gasping. 'You deserve to drown in your own mucus, you—'

'You're a sick little puppy ain't you Turow?' barked Thermidor. 'I'm kinda reluctant to admit you into my life. What about the polygraph, gumshoe? The third degree?'

'I got the word on that,' said Atom, and related the replies for the Wittgenstein control questions. These responses were a valued secret:

'Is there a hippo in the room?'

'No.'

'What evidence do you have?'

'The evidence of my senses.' (This last reply was later modified to 'Eyewitness testimony'.)

The test was intended to establish the subject's interpretational clarity and eliminate postmodern fuzz. Once the correct responses were recited, the subject was free to spout whichever nonsense he favoured. 'So there it is,' said Atom, and turned to DeCrow. 'Ever seen the read-out needles on a polygraph, Doc? Like the legs of a crushed cranefly, flickering.'

DeCrow advanced from the shadow of a corner and faced Atom across the crowded room. 'Enough,' he croaked. 'Can't you see what he's done? He's brainwashed you all! His mouth is a mecca for bullshit! How can we be cheerful with the devil among us?'

'Some people are led by an evil destiny,' said Maddy.

'Feeling left out, Doc?' Atom asked. 'DeCrow here's the

inventor of the bendy hearse, everyone. Though clearly in or perhaps beyond his declining years, he recently had a moral circuit breaker installed so that—'

'Enough, I said – if you think you can bring me here at fishpoint to listen to this garbage, you're just perhaps as mad as you pretend.'

'Go tell it to the lard mountain.'

'I intend to. And about you dispensing alibis up here, about the tank monster and that three-ring circus you call a detective agency.'

'I don't call it anything.'

'But you call yourself a detective,' snarled Turow, taking out Atom's business card. 'Or are you the "defective" Joanna said you were?'

'Take a swatch,' said Atom. 'You people came to me.'

Looking at the card, Turow was gaping like an order clown in a drive-through. Thermidor snatched it from him. 'Defective,' he read. 'What's the big idea?'

'The Candyman hired you!' squeaked Turow.

'Who said I was for hire?'

'We paid you!'

'Not me. Tough to see a bulge on Joanna, ain't it?'

'You mean . . . Joanna kept the money! Joanna!'

'Where's the galoot?' demanded Thermidor, starting about.

Atom gestured at the open door. Joanna had slipped away like a glacier. Squadcar cherrylights pulsed across the ceiling. Atom laughed low.

'You're gonna pay for this, Atom,' growled Thermidor, 'you and all your brain-eatin' friends! You used that modality and you know it!'

'K-man – gimme that little engine in your pocket.'

Kafka fished the Beretta automatic from his jacket pocket and handed it to Atom.

'The old graphic equaliser,' Atom said. 'I took it off DeCrow. But it ain't for you people. I'm a fair man.' Atom went to the drinks cabinet, put the gun on the flip-down table and backed away. 'You and me are an equal distance from the steamer, Doc – about five feet each away, I think. Take it back – I'll try to stop you.'

The ghost of a smile passed through DeCrow. 'These deceptions are perennial.'

'You don't need my blessing to think so – why tell me about it?'

'What is this shit?' roared Thermidor.

'Keep out!' shouted Atom.

A bony branch whipped from DeCrow's centre to the gun – Atom kicked upward at the fliptable, slamming it on the limb. DeCrow jettisoned the arm, shrieking as he fanned open, dropping his cover and shooting stalks and whiplike wires to the room's corners. Glimpsing a dark gut of wagging flagella and thoracic spoilers, the assembled crew began to scream like infants. DeCrow's face bivalved to hatch a wet black beak.

I am the one who is screaming the loudest, thought Sam 'Sam' Bleaker, and bolted with the other flunkeys.

Remaining in the room, Madison, Jed and K looked on as Atom retrieved the 62F and kicked aside the ditched palp. 'Here it is, DeCrow. To adopt your camouflage you had to establish what's normal around here – you never could.'

DeCrow rattled, fiddling feelers and crouching to spring. 'What are you?'

'The bluff-caller.'

Atom fired – DeCrow's head blew apart like an artillery shell, leaving a broken bowl drifting smoke. His body collapsed like a clothes rack.

The mob were bellowing down the stairwell, punching each other aside, and exploded on to the street. White light slammed on, halting them. 'You have the right to remain silent as the grave,' yelled Chief Blince. The crowd surged forward, scrabbling at Blince's sleeves and shouting plaintive yarns.

'Spandex?' said Blince. Squadlights flared like the coals of hell.

19

The Stuff that Dreams Are Made of

Sometimes Blince lay awake nights wondering who he could arrest. Tonight he was almost sated. Those morons had thrown themselves at the nets like tuna. It was damn near fantastic.

Maybe it was the extra cheese on his pasta and all but now he was dreaming of a plateau of hopscotch squares under an eye-blue sky. On each horizon was a wooden panel like a pew or jury bench. Atom rose out of the starred centre square. 'Have you hugged your gun today?'

'Atom. You gotta be kiddin'.'

'You'll get a clear description of my motives when you prise my cold dead fingers off it.'

Madison was moving around him like smoke. She raised a little injection-moulded gun. Blince chuckled. 'That a gun or an applicator?' Then it hit him and the scene went high res – behind Atom, Beerlight reared like a rolling cruise ship. 'Kinda heavy. What's it made of?'

'Well this'll interest you, Henry,' said Atom amicably. He reached way back and plucked a square brick from the city, giving it to Blince. 'Letters of the law.'

Blince looked at the ivory square with the embossed letter 'K' and found it opened into a book.

They didn't know him. They allowed their understanding to be repelled by that extrusion of his craft, the spiny carapace. The fiercest added so much scar tissue they no longer knew who they assaulted. At what time are people so reckless with meaning? When only the utterly powerful can risk an act of kindness.

'Yeah, so what's it all mean?'

'Means you don't arrest anyone in this dream here.'

'Why'd I arrest someone in a dream?'

'Exactly.'

'You're hoggin' my nightmare, boy. Why not take a trot on the water while you're at it? Think I need this?'

'No,' said Atom, and flicked a hand at the Beerlight skyline. 'You need that. Real sad.'

'Let's go, Taff,' said Maddy. 'I'm hungry.'

Beerlight started to scramble, blurring behind them. Atom stopped as they turned to go. 'Hey Henry – behavioural science got a file on me?'

'Feds maybe, since Fall Street. That's Washington stuff, Atom – they don't forget.'

'Not while they're alive. Washington's got three years. Pentagon's got five. Beerlight's got ten. You got ten, Henry. Tops. Wake up now.'

The alarm rang like a cigarette burn.

'So Flea, you stole that apple?'

'Maybe,' muttered Flea, uncomfortable. He nursed a glowing glass of Chile Mars 96.

'Flea,' said Madison, sat on the corner of Atom's desk, 'that lighter you sold me damn near took my head off. Now why don't I trust you?'

'I don't know, I'm conflicted,' said Flea. 'Got carried away with the publicity. Told Specter I climbed the wall near the applecart using my ears as suction cups.'

'But to ascend you'd have to take one ear from the

134

surface and turn your head a hundred and eighty degrees to attach the other one – you'd fall right away.'

'That's what the judge said during his charge to the jury. Okay, maybe I didn't think it through. I forgot people can be identified by an earprint – the cops tested the wall.'

'Didn't find anything, eh?' asked Atom.

'They found hundreds of earprints but none of 'em were mine. Specter was real mad.'

'Well, the cops want a barbecue, Flea.' Atom lit Maddy's shock absorber. 'You don't carry enough weight to flip a slide door. Why'd you lay this down?'

'The Twins put a bee in my head about not bein' a perp. I wanted to prove somethin'. Turns out they'd already left town – gone to Washington.'

'Their kinda felony's arterial, Flea – quantum innovation. You ain't that kinda cross-grained mark. Why should you be?'

'So I guess Fiasco's gonna buzz again,' said Madison. 'Come on, Taff, let's get to the beach.'

Atom and Drowner carried Jed's tank through the waiting room. The floor-to-ceiling wall painting was now a lurid menagerie of bleak-featured panthers, ants, scorpions, skeletons, string-trailing brains like man-o'-war jellyfish, deaf bees, giant rabbits and blissed-out turtles. The tucked coral of gowny seas, peace and ocean draping through wrecked fibres. Here was an owl with a face like an intake fan, there a city father lying helpless as a flipped bug. Children tapped at earthquake lids. A raven watched it all, allowing its consequence as elsewhere a landscape thrived. Green water meadows. Scattering rain. A field sprouting a whole new colour, part head and part heart.

Kitty had a makeover. She returned to *Vogue* and ran the gamut, following every tip. By the end, her few remnants of character had been utterly extinguished. There was nothing in the mirror.

A half-hour later, ten thousand dollars simply disappeared from the register at the Chain Bank. An hour after that, a guard fell abruptly unconscious in the uptown den. Another one went to help and slammed suddenly to the floor. A ring of keys lifted off his belt, drifted toward a cell door and jangled in place – the door swung.

Sitting calm on a bunk, Harry Fiasco looked up without surprise. His face brightened into a smile.

Madison sunbathed like a photograph. Atom lay reading *Investigations of a Dog* as Tamagotchi Bloodbath played on the radio. The author had complained of the brightening weather and Atom had set him up in one of the new burrow homes off the old subway. 'Live long,' K had said, 'and may all admire you for stubbornly maintaining such a hideous mistake.'

'There's just a thousand things I don't understand,' said Jed Helms, sticking his face out of the tank, 'but the main one is, how did you know DeCrow was a human brain in a bug's body, and not the other way around?'

Atom lowered the book, squinting aside. 'Well the Candyman suggested he'd performed one or other of those operations, but DeCrow emanated spite of a rare purity – something only God or humanity can achieve. The brain had to be human, and the body that of a chigger. Funny when you realise an itch is an insect. And I never credited Joanna. That kinda luck's as rare as a hog's hesitation. They still ain't found him.'

'I . . . I guess I'm ready, Atom,' said Jed.

Madison stirred, and exchanged a look with Atom. They stood up and lifted the tank, carrying it the little way to the waves. 'Knock 'em dead,' said Atom.

136

They decanted Jed into the rolling surf. 'It's cold,' he said, turning pale. 'Wow, it's big.' And he wagged his tail, slowly moving away without a backward glance.

'Sweet dreams, Jed,' said Madison.

'How long will he last?'

'I don't know.'

They returned to the beach blankets, dropping down. Atom put on his shades – the sky turned the colour of gasoline. Something was missing – a link. He waited, patient as time.

The Tamagotchi track ended and Perky Gumbubble started yammering. 'We're privileged to welcome the President of the United States. Mr President, over the past few days your actions have caused massive speculation. It seems you've undergone a fundamental change of image. After controversial incidents with dogs, lizards, squid, snakes and a defenceless manatee called Ramone, is this a deliberate overhaul? And have you been instrumental in the escalation of the nuclear programme?'

A blubbery laugh bubbled over the airwaves. 'That I am, sir, that I am. I admire a man sir who admires a man sir who admires a man sir, that I do sir.'

For a while the sea and seagulls clamoured in their ears. Then Atom smiled thoughtfully. 'I guess the Twins had the right idea.'

'Haven't been to DC in a while. We welcome?'

Atom stood, squinting towards the car. 'Fuck 'em if they can't take a joke.'

Madison joined him, smirking like a shark. 'What if they can?'

They started to walk. 'Fuck 'em anyway.'